# THERESE GREENWOOD

# KILL
# AS YOU
# GO

# THERESE GREENWOOD

# KILL
# AS YOU
# GO

♣ ◆ ♠ ♥

To George
With thanks, and the
greatest affection, for
the years of interesting
conversations,

COFFIN HOP PRESS LTD.
CANADA

Cheers
"TG"

Copyright © 2018 by Therese Greenwood
Edited by Robert Bose and Axel Howerton

**Wrecked** - originally published in *Ellery Queen Mystery Magazine*, March-April 2012.

**A Jury of Her Peers** - originally published in *Bloody Words The Anthology,* Baskerville Books, 2003.

**A Way With Horses** - originally published in *Ellery Queen Mystery Magazine*, Sept-Oct. 2004.

**Kill As You Go** - originally published as *A Little Bit Easy* in *When Boomers Go Bad*, Rendezvous Press, Summer 2005.

**Fair Lady** - originally published in *Menopause is Murder*, Ladies Killing Circle, 2000

**A Christmas Bauble** - originally published in *The Kingston Whig-Standard*, December 2003

**Sister Companion** - originally published in *Over The Edge,* Crime Writers of Canada, 2000.

**Dr. Spankie's Car** - originally published in *Sun Media Summer Mystery Festival*, Sun Media Group, 2003.

**Crown Witness** - originally published in *Sun Media Summer Mystery Festival*, Sun Media, 2006.

**Holding Down The Fort** - originally published in *Cottage Country Killers*, General Store Publishing, 1997.

All rights reserved. No part of this publication may be reproduced, distributed or transmitted in any form or by any means, including photocopying, recording, or other electronic or mechanical methods, without the prior written permission of the publisher, except in the case of brief quotations embodied in critical reviews and certain other noncommercial uses permitted by copyright law. For permission requests, write to the publisher at the address below.

**Coffin Hop Press**
200 Rivervalley Crescent SE
Calgary, Alberta CANADA T2C 3K8
www.coffinhop.com
mailto:info@coffinhop.com

A Proudly Canadian Publisher

Cover Design ©2018 Coffin Hop Press
Cover element: **lukeruk** Shutterstock ID: 702758095
Book Layout ©2018 Coffin Hop Press

Kill As You Go/Therese Greenwood —1st ed. Paperback
ISBN: 978-1-988987-06-4

*For my sisters*
*Cathy, Kim and Annette,*
*who listened to my stories.*

*"I guess I can put two and two together."*

*"Sometimes the answer's four," I said,*
*"and sometimes it's twenty-two."*

— Dashiell Hammett, *The Thin Man*

# CONTENTS

# *Introduction*

**Back in the late '80s and early '90s**, I edited a few collections of short Canadian crime fiction. It was a tough time for short stories, as it usually is, and lots of unsolicited material was coming in from lots of people. For a while, it seemed like stories were showing up in the mail every day.  Some of them were pretty good and some, well…

Then one day, several years ago I was doing a reading in Belleville, Ontario, and a young woman approached me with a story she asked me to consider.  She was funny and articulate and worked doing PR for a bunch of nuns.  There could be few better qualifications than that.

The story Therese Greenwood gave me that evening was called "Sister Companion." It still is called that, as far as I know, and I read it with delight. It's a highly entertaining story about a highwayman, theft, duplicity, and nuns. They say you should write what you know.

9

The story was purchased, basically without any editing at all, and was included in a Crime Writers of Canada anthology called *Over the Edge*, published in 2000 by Pottersfield Press.

Since then, Therese has been busy. She helped found the Scene of the Crime mystery writing festival on her native Wolfe Island. She co-edited the Osprey Summer Mystery Series for a few years in the early 2000s. She edited a couple of anthologies. She was published in Ellery Queen Mystery Magazine, the holy grail for mystery short story writers. And she wrote a lot more stories.

Many of Therese's stories are historical, some featuring John A. Macdonald as a detective, finding time to solve crimes while building a nascent country. Many are set on Wolfe Island, which clearly harbours more than its share of dark secrets. Some have been nominated for Arthur Ellis Awards.

Maybe one of the reasons I like Therese's work is that her sense of what makes good writing is the same as mine. No wasted words. No needless descriptions. No inane dialogue. Just good, solid, sharp, tight, entertaining storytelling.

Oh yeah, and Therese also knows when to use adjectives and when not to.

Peter Sellers
Author, Editor

# KILL AS YOU GO

# A Way With Horses

**Sheldon Blacklock had been sitting** on top of the hay wagon for a good half hour. It gave him the best view across the St. Lawrence River to the American town on the opposite shore and he saw Kit the instant she strolled across the main street and onto the big dock at Telegraph Point. Even with the quarter mile of busy shipping channel between them, boats rushing across the border with lumber and grain and people, he was sure it was Kit. There wasn't another woman for a hundred miles who wore a red dress on a Tuesday afternoon. Kit didn't save colours for Saturday nights, she adorned her big curves with reds and purples and yellows like a crazy painting

Sheldon had seen in a lawyer's office in town. She would be extra dolled up today because of their plan, the rest of her beads and frippery packed for Syracuse and points south.

The furthest south Sheldon had ever been was the town he was looking at, Cape Vincent, New York, with its frame houses and hay dealers and grocers who could tell you the day the town got electric lights. His earliest memory was of standing here on Horne's Point, the south-ernmost tip of the big Canadian island around which Lake Ontario spilled into the St. Lawrence River. Even then he dreamed of leaving the island for New York, Philadelphia, Boston and Miami, cities he read about in dime novels, where Prohibition made life even faster and things went on day and night. Where he was heading now that Kit had waved the go-ahead signal with one brash move, not re-peated because she was sure he was looking. The sun glinted on her silver compact as she turned away to pow-der her nose.

"Put your eyes back in your head," said Maddy. He had been looking at Kit so hard he scarcely heard his sister-in-law and his brother Everett pull up the buggy at the end of the island's longest road.

"Just admiring the view," said Sheldon, sliding from the top of the wagon, careful not to dislodge the well-packed bales. He was careful, too, of the loaded pistol in his jacket pocket, the one the man from Ogdensburg had given him the day they shot forty-two mallards.

"I know what you're admiring," said Maddy, "and I don't know what you see in it." She thought Kit was Jezebel, Salome and Gloria Swanson rolled into one. All the island, even Everett, thought the same but she was the only one who would say it. To think he had been half in love with Maddy, a slip of a thing with snapping blue eyes and a sharp tongue. He and Everett had taken turns dancing with her to Katie Greenwood's victrola and partnering her at the euchre games at the church hall. Then Sheldon started guiding the Americans who came north looking for small-mouth bass and pike in the summer and Canada geese and wood duck in the fall. The hunters woke with a shot of whiskey and spent the day polishing off as much drink as wildlife and talking about the three things that mattered, guns, women and whiskey. The Canadian sidewalks rolled up early and at night Sheldon ferried the Americans back to the Cape for poker and corn liquor, and he met Kit at The Anchor. She was nothing like Maddy. She had brass and laughed like a man while she matched him shot for shot of Jack Daniels, then used quick, wide slashes to replace her bright red Luxor lip pomade. Sheldon smuggled her bottles of Corby's rye and Kit would laugh her man laugh and say she went for the strong Canadian stuff. Everybody knew she didn't mean booze.

"When are you going to grow up, Sheldon?" Maddy scolded, the palm of her hand cupped over the swell of her belly where her first baby was growing. It was fine for his brother to settle down at twenty years of age, fenced in with a church-going wife and baby and thirty acres of

15

passable pasture. Everett didn't have the mind's eye for anything bigger than an island eleven miles long. But Sheldon wouldn't say that out loud, not in front of his brother.

"Shel, you should've waited for me to load the wagon," said Everett, handing Maddy the lines and jumping off the bench seat, landing lightly on the balls of his feet. To do business in the Cape he wore his Sunday suit, the one Maddy hand-made for him, even the tie, and his thick black hair was slicked down, making him look like a kid off to Sunday school.

"I needed to get moving," said Sheldon. He'd loaded the big wagon before the crack of dawn and maybe he'd hitched the team too early, for the horses had picked up on his nerves and were fidgeting in the traces.

"We ought to make two trips, take the team and then the wagon," said Everett, giving the horses a once-over, running his hands along the harness, careful not get horse snot on his clothes. "Tony's a little frisky."

"That colt is as green as a grasshopper," snapped Maddy. Tony was only broke to harness on the island, where there were no stop lights or trains and only a dozen cars, all of which pulled over if they saw Blacklock's green colt. But the big problem was the middle of river and Maddy knew it. "If Tony gets spooked on the barge he'll take the wagon, the old mare and everything else straight to the bottom." Kit would have said straight to hell.

"Now Maddy, you know Ev can handle any horse," said Sheldon, surprised to hear pride in his voice. "He's like those cowboys in the pictures at the Bijou, who get horses

16

to drag them out of quicksand. Anyways, we don't have time for two trips. The train will be at the station in half an hour and we got to load up before it pulls out."

"We best get going," said Everett, cutting off Maddy's next remark by reaching both hands for the wax-paper-wrapped sandwich she was holding. As he took it he held her hand a little longer than necessary and gave it a squeeze. Sheldon had never seen them touch, not since they kissed at the altar, and he felt ashamed of noticing.

"I made enough for you too, Sheldon," Maddy said, still looking at his brother. "Everett would share his with you anyway." Then she flicked the lines over the pony's back and turned back down the road. "Watch yourselves," she called out over her shoulder.

"A lot of fuss over a ten-minute barge ride," Sheldon grumbled.

"What can go wrong?" Everett asked as he leapt onto the wagon's bench seat, the hay towering over him. Of course, he didn't know the hay was piled two bales thick around ten thousand dollars worth of Corby's whiskey. He didn't know, either, that smuggling the whiskey to the States was where he came in. Everett really was like those movie cowboys. He never took a drop of liquor, never missed church on Sunday, had never uttered a swearword in his life. Even now, with Pa dead almost six months and no one to live up to any more, Everett was a rootin'-tootin' good guy. And he was never, ever, searched by the excise men on the other side of the river.

Everett drove the team down the cement incline of the boat ramp with a touch on the lines, calling something Sheldon couldn't hear. The barge was smallish, just a half-foot bigger around than the wagon and team, and Tony twitched in the tight space until Everett gave the lines another touch and spoke again.

Sheldon climbed aboard and started the motor, the one from the old Chevy truck engine, and it put-putted away as he eased them out into the channel. The wind was up and there was a bit of chop, the water always ran faster on this side of the island, but things went smooth enough for the first hundred yards until the American patrol boat came up out of nowhere.

They called it a six-bitter, for the half-dozen machine guns mounted along its 75-foot sides. They didn't even count the one-pound, rapid-fire gun that swivelled to fire in any direction. Sheldon counted it though, he counted the patrol boat a floating nightmare. Grey as fog and built for the ocean, it had come up the river hunting bootleggers from Detroit and Chicago, the big-time gangsters stealing up from the Great Lakes. Sheldon supposed the gun power must be working because lately he hadn't seen any out-of-town thugs in the speakeasies on the wrong side of the Cape's railway tracks.

But would they turn that gun power on him? The barge was still on the Canadian side of the river and if Sheldon turned back now the patrol boat couldn't follow, not legally. He looked back at Everett, who was keeping an eye on the wake the American boat churned up. Then Sheldon

18

looked ahead to Kit, still standing on the point, and she waved with both arms, urging him to her. If he turned back the G-men would know something was up and he wouldn't get another chance at a stake that would take Kit out of the town too small to hold her.

As the barge sliced across the invisible border the patrol boat changed course towards them and someone on the bridge gave Sheldon the sign to cut his engine. He threw the switch and the barge pitched in the boat's wake. Everett sang out in his soothing voice but Tony snorted and jerked, lifting one big hoof after another, rocking the wagon back and forth so that one of the top bales tumbled off and into the water. The splash spooked Tony and it spooked Sheldon, too, because that left only one bale between the whiskey and the patrol boat. He put his hand in his jacket pocket and felt the pistol grip, cold as a stone.

Everett slipped off the wagon seat and made his way to front of the barge, graceful as a girl as he sidestepped the stamping hoofs. Everett was a small man although Sheldon seldom thought of him that way. He didn't think of himself as small and he and Everett were much of a size, thin and wiry with almost dainty features. Everett looked even smaller as he took off his jacket, his shirt white as snow, the billowy sleeves held up by garters on his forearms. He wrapped the coat around Tony's eyes. Maddy would give him hell.

"Everett Blacklock, as I live and breathe," said a voice from the patrol boat. Sheldon shielded his eyes with his palm and looked up into the sun, recognizing one of the Cape Vincent excise men.

"How've you been keeping?" said Everett in his calm, smooth voice, one hand stroking the colt's neck.

Sheldon silently cursed his brother's obliging nature and tightened his hold on the gun. His palms were sweaty, the pistol grip had gone damp, and he wondered if he had the nerve to shoot his way out.

"Fair to middling," said the excise man. "Yourself?"

"Never better," said Everett. The horse jerked his head up hard and would have smashed Everett in the chin if he hadn't stepped aside in time.

Sheldon wondered how far he would make it if he jumped into the lake and swam for Canadian water. Maybe they wouldn't go too hard on Everett. The worst they would give him was three years, if he got a wet judge.

"Everett Blacklock is the most honest man in two counties." The excise man turned to the ship's captain, who took his hand from the sidearm strapped to his hip and looked a tad disappointed. "We'd best let him get on about his business."

"Be seeing you," said Everett politely, waving with one hand, still stroking the horse's neck with the other.

The patrol boat pulled away slowly, taking care not to throw up much backwash. Everett kept Tony blindfolded and the horse stayed more or less calm as Sheldon started the motor. They didn't have far to go and Sheldon's heart almost stopped racing by the time they docked at the wharf where Kit stood waiting, hands on her hips.

"My sweet lord, Shellie," she called as he cut the engine and aimed the barge plumb at the boat ramp. No one else called him Shellie but it didn't sound small from her. "When those G-men pulled up next to you I just about had kittens."

"Friends of Everett," he said, tossing her the tie rope.

"Everett has a friendly side?" sassed Kit, wrapping the rope around the cleat and giving him a bold view down the front of her dress. He stepped off the barge and she jumped into his arms, wrapping her arms and legs around him and kissing him till her lipstick was all over his cheek. Now Everett would see how a woman showed a man she loved him. But when a breathless Sheldon turned around Everett was going about his business, leading the team off the barge and through the customs check, the excise men waving him past.

"There goes Mr. Friendly," Kit said, her bosom still heaving.

Everett didn't speak a word to Kit when Sheldon handed her into the wagon and climbed up after her. Kit stuck close as a whisper to Sheldon, touching him, sighing in his ear, rubbing against him, while a silent Everett drove up the empty street to the Rome-Watertown line. Sheldon was preoccupied, partly with Kit's carrying on and partly wondering what his brother would do when he saw the real goods. Maybe Everett would keep looking away, the way he did when Kit put her hand up high on Sheldon's thigh. But he never found out what Everett would have done because they no sooner pulled up the wagon than the man with the tommy gun stepped out between the horses and the train tracks.

"Hand 'er over, hayseed," said the tommy gun.

Sheldon had seen him at the Anchor once or twice, a big operator from Detroit with a silk suit and a loud city tie. Sheldon slid his hand down behind Kit's back and slipped it into his jacket pocket. He couldn't make a move though, not with Kit in the line of fire.

"I expect he's after that whiskey you hid inside the bales," said Everett.

Sheldon didn't register it then, that Everett knew all along; he was still wondering how the gangster had cottoned on to it.

"You'd better hand it over, Shellie," said Kit. "He means business."

Everett left the lines on the seat and carefully slid to the ground, taking a cautious step back from the wagon. Sheldon turned to Kit, thinking to get her off the wagon fast and out of harm's way before he made his stand.

"Sorry, Shellie." She took out her compact and looked at herself in the mirror, dabbing lip pomade against her full bottom lip with her little finger. "I'm staying for the ride."

"You stupid bumpkin," said the tommy gun. "What's a woman like that going to do with a yokel like you?"

"Kit?" Sheldon didn't like the question in his voice but he couldn't help it, it gasped out of the hole opening up in his gut.

Kit laughed her man laugh, the one he thought so fine. She smacked her lips, looked in the compact mirror and said, "You screwed your own brother, Shellie, now which one of us is worse?"

She was right. That's what Sheldon thought when he pulled out the gun and pointed it between her red lips. She gave him a surprised smile, her eyebrows raised.

"I wouldn't," said tommy gun, "unless you want me to blow your brother's head off."

In the dime novels they called it a Mexican standoff but it didn't feel like they described it. Sheldon's gaze wasn't steely, his hands shook like a butter churn, and for a nasty moment he thought he would wet himself. It felt like a life went by in a lazy swish of Tony's tail, guns pointed at the only two people he had loved, and then the train whistle sounded.

"Train's coming," said Everett in the soft voice he used with horses.

Sheldon felt his grip on the gun loosen and he turned from Kit to toss it to the ground. Then he slid off the wagon but he didn't step back like his brother. Instead he looked up at Kit one last time as she snapped her compact shut, tossed it in her bag, and shimmied over to let tommy gun hop up next to her.

"Nothing personal, Shellie," said Kit, putting her hand high on the inside of tommy gun's thigh.

"The train," began Everett but Sheldon drew back his hand and slapped Tony hard on the rump, sending the team off at a good clip across the tracks. Tommy gun

23

reached forward to collect the trailing lines and Everett took a few steps forward, calling something after them, his voice lost in the sound of the train.

They used to call trains iron horses, that went through Sheldon's mind as it happened. He could never picture the crash, exactly how it looked as Tony bolted and over-turned the wagon on the tracks. He only remembered the sound, the crunching, grinding mess of steel hitting bone and wood and whiskey. It was so loud he never heard Kit scream. Maybe she never had time. But he could hear a horse screaming, people yelling, the steam engine hissing, and the bells of the fire engine as it raced up the street even though there was no fire.

A single bottle of whiskey rolled to a stop at Sheldon's feet, somehow unbroken, a little miracle. He uncorked it and tipped the neck high over his head so the liquor burned straight down his throat. When he lowered the bottle Everett was picking up the pistol and checking the load in the chamber, flicking it shut with a sideways flick like a cowboy. Sheldon took another swig of whiskey and Everett reached out a hand that held the soft linen hand-kerchief Maddy had sewn.

"You got lipstick on your face," Everett said.

Sheldon took another slug of the Corby's and Everett put the hankie back in his pocket and turned to the wreck. Sheldon had never seen Everett with a pistol but he seemed to know the gun, holding it loosely at his side as he knelt beside Tony, dodging the sharp, flashing hooves and stroking the straining neck for a last second. The single shot went straight into the horse's brain and there was a little less noise.

The horse's blood marked the front of Everett's coat in a stain so deep Maddy would never get it out. He dabbed at it with his handkerchief as he headed to the dock, holding the gun like a hammer and passing Sheldon with no more of a look than he would give a fencepost. When Everett reached Telegraph Point he pulled back his arm and, in the only angry gesture Sheldon had seen his brother make, hurled the pistol into deep water.

Sheldon drained the last of the whiskey, the marks of the woman's lips still on his face, as he watched his brother cross the river home.

# Fair Lady

The geese stopped honking when the corn landed at their feet. In the sudden calm, Emily Munn could hear the buzz of the boat her husband had built. The Fair Lady was humming its old familiar tune as it skipped across Big Sandy Bay and Emily wished for the hundredth time that it was bringing Joe home.

In an hour the sun would be peeking over the surface of the St. Lawrence, the morning air full of the bracing river scent, and Joe should be striding up the path from the dock with Rolly close behind, both of them teasing her by whistling the "old grey goose is dead," like they always did when they caught her at the goose pen. But Joe was down in the States doing three years and a day for running whisky, while their son haunted the old farm like the ghosts who had followed him home from Vimy Ridge. Sometimes it seemed like the only one left from before the Great War was the blessed grey goose. She turned the old bucket upside over the top of the pen and dumped the last bit of feed right on top of the old bird. It gave a sharp honk, shivered it off, and went right back to scratching the feed from the dusty earth of the pen.

Emily wiped her hands on the boys' knickers she always wore when she was doing chores and turned to Rolly standing guard at the goose pen gate. He had stood at silent attention while she did her chores, rifle at the ready, shoulders back, chest out, his muddy uniform existing only in his maimed mind. In fact his shirt and pants were clean as a whistle; just yesterday she had washed and hung them on the line, but their fresh fragrance escaped him. To think she had been so happy when she had heard he was going in for the medical corps and not the regular fighting.

"Bud Henley's coming in," Emily said. "I can hear the boat."

"Will there be many wounded?" Rolly asked. He spoke in that calm tone he always used when he was having one of his spells, the tone Emily found so spooky because it seemed like his fear was buried a thousand miles away in a Flanders trench.

"There's been no battle, son," she answered.

28

"Sergeant Jones said there was something in the wind just before he headed out after the last deserter. Jonesie's never wrong."

"Don't fret, son. I'll go on down and meet Bud. Then maybe he won't smash into the dock again."

It was hard making all the decisions with Joe gone and her alone for the first time in twenty-seven years. They wouldn't be in this fix if she hadn't let Rolly try to take over Joe's liquor run, but he had been so long without a spell and Lord knew they needed the money. They had spent every cent on that Yankee lawyer, the one who didn't know his rear-end from a hole in the ground.

The Fair Lady had no running lights but Emily could hear the engine running a bit cranky as it pulled in towards the dock. Joe had put an old Chevy engine in the St. Lawrence skiff. He claimed it was faster than the Model T motors the other rum runners used, but it was a cantankerous piece of work and you had to have a feel for it. Bud Henley had no feel for it. He was coming in too fast and she'd mention it if he scraped into the dock again. Sure enough, Bud did not ease up on the throttle in time, slamming the twenty-six feet of sturdy wooden boat into the weather-beaten dock that had to be rebuilt every spring because of the damage from the winter ice. He cut the engine, thrusting aside the gingham curtain Emily had sewn to separate the tiny wheelhouse from the rear of the home-made skiff. There was a heavy scowl on his young face and he made a move as if he might tear down the wisp of material.

"Mornin' Bud," Emily said. Then, to remind him that, for now at least, the Fair Lady was her property, she added, "You'd best take care when you bring her into the dock."

He ignored her words as he tossed her the boat's line. "The booze ain't out there. Either somebody got to it or that fool boy of yours gave me the wrong directions."

"Are you sure?" she asked as she gave the line a quick double loop around the dock's iron ring, the one Joe had cemented into place two summers ago.

"You don't see any booze, do you?"

"You must've missed the spot," Emily said, but it was obvious Bud should have had no problem snagging the rum line. It was a calm night, the lake was like glass, and there was lots of moonlight. It was the perfect night to snag the ten burlap sacks, one case of hooch per, tied together for exactly the kind of emergency that had made Rolly drop them over the side of the boat.

"I was in the right spot. Big Al's dock was at one end of the bay, the Stanley's silo at the other. Exactly like that moron said." Bud began to coil the old chain he had been dragging back and forth along the bay, one end lashed to a rusty propeller. The propeller should have caught on the rum line, bringing the rope and the sacks linked to it to the surface. He folded the chain end over end, wrapping it from thumb to elbow in a bundle that would store under one of the rough pine benches that ran down the sides of the skiff. "So who'd you tell about it? You women can't keep nothing quiet."

"I never told a soul but you, Bud."

"Well it ain't there.

"You should've taken me out with you."

"Bootleggin' ain't a job for a female." He placed the chain under the bench, preserving its coil so it would slip easily into the water the next time. "Women ain't making any money off Prohibition, at least not standing up, and I don't expect you'd make much in that line. Not exactly a fair lady, are you?"

She wanted to cuff him, knocking that silly little cloth cap he fancied so much floating into the bay. But the people from Syracuse knew Bud worked with Joe whenever Rolly took a spell, and they certainly didn't want to deal with a woman. Now Bud was edging her and Rolly all the way out and he wasn't taking his time about it, either. "You think about my offer to buy the boat, Emily?" he asked.

"That's Mrs. Munn to you."

"Em – Mrs. Munn, there's a load from Belleville coming in tonight. Even with the rumline gone, I can make sure you and Rolly get looked after."

"Like you looked after Joe?"

It was a sore point but Bud went for a coaxing tone. "Now Mrs. Munn, everybody knows you have to watch your back in this business. When those G-men come running onto the dock Joe was unlucky he was all the way down in the unloading shed. They'd have got us both if I hadn't hit the engine so fast, and if both Joe and I was in jail they'd have taken the Fair Lady, too. Then where would you be, with your boy laid up? Up shit creek with no sign of a paddle."

"Watch your language," Emily said.

"Time's wasting and there's money to be made," Bud said, unoffended. "We got a big shipment off the train two nights ago and the one-lungers ferried it up to the cove. They ain't fast enough to cross the border and we got word the customs is getting close. We gotta bring it in to-night and unless Rolly comes out of the shellshock today I'm the only one that can handle the job."

"We best head up to the house and sort it out."

As they headed up the path towards the goose pen, Emily thought what an unlikely pair they would look if Rol-ly could see their real faces. Her features were as weather-worn as the old farmhouse, showing every one of her for-ty-six years and a few she hadn't even lived yet. Even in the dark Bud's arrogant young face had a glow to it, shin-ing underneath his yellow cap, his gait jaunty as he saw himself stepping up in the world. He was a tad younger than Rolly, young enough to have missed the Great War, but then the War wouldn't have cut him up the way it did her son. Bud was ten degrees cooler than a cucumber. Look how he'd bided his time, with "Yes, Mr. Munn" and "No, Mr. Munn," doing all the toady jobs on the boat until Joe's jailing and Rolly's setback brought him crawling out of the woodwork to take over the Fair Lady, the only thing she had that could possibly make them a living.

They got close to the edge of the pen before the geese heard them coming and let out a racket to wake the dead.

Over the din Rolly called out, "Advance and be recognized," and the grin disappeared from Bud's face as he made out Rolly's ram-rod straight silhouette. It was funny how the sight of a man gone off his head made other men want to run, like it was a disease they might catch.

"Just what the hell do you think you're doing?" Bud yelled over the blaring honks.

"The captain said everyone on stretcher detail had to take a turn at guarding the deserters."

"Is there no way you can stop that hullabaloo?"

"The shelling sure gets to you sometimes," said Rolly. "The sergeant says that's what makes men bolt, the sound drives them mad."

Bud moved too close to the fence and as the old grey goose snapped at him, he turned accusingly to Emily. "Why don't you wring that old buzzard's neck and be done with it? She don't lay no more, she's no good for eatin'."

"There's some life in the old girl yet," said Emily, turning to Rolly. "Come along, son. Another fellow's going to take over your watch for a bit."

The kitchen was warm from the cookstove Emily had lit as soon as she had awakened. It was a big stove, bought the first year of her marriage when she thought she'd be cooking for a dozen instead of the one child the Lord had seen fit to send her. The two pots she always left on the stove were at a light simmer, one ready for potatoes or soup or greens, the second the big enamel teapot that was never allowed to run dry. Joe liked his tea strong enough to stand a spoon up in and long years of habit had her keep the pot simmering as if he might walk in any moment. She pushed the teapot to the front of the stove to bring it to a boil, then spoke to Rolly before she lit the lamp. He had panicked once, thinking the light would draw the Huns' fire. "We've got the black-out on the windows," she said, then filled the kitchen with the glow from the oil lamp.

"It's been a hungry night's work," said Bud, keeping the yellow cap on his head as he took Joe's seat at the head of the pine harvest table. "Fix us up some breakfast."

Emily pulled a piece of split wood from the six-foot pile she kept behind the stove, opened the oven door and used the stick to poke the fire before adding it to the blaze. Bud was behind her, speaking as if Rolly wasn't in the room. "Faint heart never won fair lady," Bud said. He must have liked the sound of that because he repeated it. "Faint heart never won fair lady and Rolly's heart ain't never going to be too steady. He ain't in no condition for this kind of work. There's always some temperance bastard tipping off the customs, and then the shootin' starts."

Rolly piped up. "The shooting never stops. Buried ten men last night." He shivered and brushed at a spot of Flanders mud on his clean shirt. "But I'd rather bury them than dig them out of stink holes. It took a dozen of us to pull out the sergeant night before last. He was in so deep I thought we'd be sucked in with him."

Bud looked at Emily triumphantly as she put steaming mugs of tea on the table, then he shovelled three spoons of her hard-bought sugar and a generous dollop of cream into his cup. Thank God the Murphys had been sending over the extra from their cow since Joe got into his trouble, she thought as she reached into the pantry for the last of the bacon. She was slicing the meat into strips and dropping it into the pan when Bud renewed his attack. "You know I got that deal set up for tonight. All I need is the boat and everything is sweet."

"I could handle that load till Rolly gets back on his feet," Emily said. She moved the faded tea towel from the basket of eggs, selecting half a dozen brown ones which she dropped into the spitting bacon without losing a yolk.

"Mrs. Munn, do you think Joe would want you out on the river?"

"Joe ain't here and all he left behind is that flat piece of driftwood that ain't much good for anything but running booze." She scooped the eggs and bacon out onto the plates and set them in front of the two young men.

"Thanks cookie," Rolly said. "I don't know how you do it on these rations but every now and then your feed puts me in mind of my ma's back home."

Emily laid a third plate of eggs and bacon down on the table, then went back to the stove and scraped the pan, pouring the hot bacon grease into the drippings can. "Ain't you going to sit down to your plate?" Bud asked as she ignored the third plate on the table.

"That's Sergeant Jones's plate," Rolly said.

"I never heard of no Jones," said Bud.

"He's out looking for the last deserter," Rolly said. "He caught some stretcher bearers hiding out in a blockhouse

35

yesterday and blew his top after all the carrying we'd been doing, through the mud and barbed wire till we couldn't hardly take another step. He used his rifle to rout them to the forward zone, but four of them flat out said no. We got three back in the stockade but the last one got away. Jonesie went out after him. It's bad for morale when they start slipping away like that."

"Morale or not, you're in trouble," said Bud. "Somebody has got to haul that load."

"I volunteer, sir," said Rolly. He stood up and carried his empty plate over to his mother at the sink. "I'd rather go over the top than pick up any more bodies."

For two beats of Emily's heart there was silence and then she took the plate from his hands. "Sergeant Jones told you to keep an eye on those deserters. You got your orders and you'd best get back out to your post."

"Yes, sir." Rolly picked up the rifle he had leaned against the table.

"You best be on the lookout," Bud added maliciously. "I hear they're deserting all over the place."

"I'll keep a close eye," Rolly said as he walked out into the dawning light.

Emily went to the stove's reservoir to scoop out a basin of hot water for the dirty dishes. She took the soap bar from beside the sink and sliced some shavings into the basin, then worked the hand pump at the sink to add some cold water. Bud was wiping up the last of the eggs. "They'll pay me off at the end of tonight's delivery and I'll give you the price of the boat. I don't expect the old tub is worth much."

"It's worth a hundred dollars a night when it's full of booze."

"Well Emily, it don't look like you're in much of a position to bargain." Bud stood up, slapped the crumbs from his lap, then strode out slamming the screen door behind him. Emily watched the wooden door flap back a time or two before blowing out the lamp. There was no sense wasting oil. There was no sense wasting good food either, not with things so tight, so she sat down at Sergeant Jones' cooling plate of eggs. She was just lifting her fork when the raised voices came to her. She went out onto the porch for a look and saw the morning sun had wrapped its fingers around the two young men who stood arguing out on the dock, one annoyed and anxious, one chillingly calm.

"Halt and show your pass," Rolly said, his rifle slung across his shoulder as he faced Bud on the dock, blocking the way to the Fair Lady.

"Bugger off," Bud said, pushing past and striding to the end of the dock with the determined young soldier dogging his steps, their hollow footfalls ringing out on the worn planks. Bud looked nervous and his hands fumbled as he tugged at the boatline, finally slipping it loose and jumping aboard the Fair Lady. Emily wondered if the north wind would help him as the boat drifted off and it did seem to give him a bit of a head start. The Fair Lady was about six yards from the dock when Bud got down on his hands and knees to roll over her engine. All it needed to start was a sharp pull, straight out, but he had no feel for it. One try, two tries, three tries, nothing, and Rolly called again for him to halt. The boat had only drifted another three yards when Rolly brought his weapon to his shoulder and took aim, calling "Stop in the name of the King."

"You and the King can go to hell," Bud yelled in a high voice that reminded Emily how young he was. She saw his frantic cranking stop for a minute as he turned to the house, and there was relief in his voice as he called out to her. "Mrs. Munn, call your crazy boy off!" Emily stood silently, and Bud redoubled his efforts to spark the engine.

Rolly's first shot came through the wheelhouse curtain she had sewn to protect Joe from the winds. She saw it drift back a bit as though in a small breeze. With the second shot Bud tripped backwards from the tiny cabin, staggering towards the stern. He hung over the side for a fraction of a moment, his yellow hat toppling into the water before he did. Emily wondered how many men Rolly had seen die, had killed like that, hung up for a minute between this world and the next. She had thought Bud would sink – Rolly had talked of bodies sinking into mudholes – but instead he floated, finally bare-headed, arms outstretched, a surprisingly thin red stain swirling along behind him in the boat's eddy. Rolly jumped in to tug the body back to shore, pulling it up, not on the dock, but onto the dirt and seaweed of the shore. He stood there a minute, looking down at it, then shouldered his weapon and walked up towards Emily. The geese went into their usual frenzy as he walked past their pen but he paid them no mind.

"I wish to report I have shot a deserter." He snapped a salute as he walked up onto the porch.

"Yes," she said, her voice sounding like Rolly's.

"Awaiting orders, sir."

In the end, she had him dig up the goose pen to get the burlap bags of hooch they had hidden there the night before last. The geese put up a ferocious racket as they dug, the old grey nipping at their heels, but Rolly didn't seem to notice them and Emily could hold no malice. That crankiness made them such good watchdogs, and once you got used to it the noise faded into the background like an enemy bombardment that didn't quite reach the ranks.

As they hauled the burlap sacks from the earth and slung them into the home-made stretcher she could see why Rolly thought each had been a dead comrade when he had helped her plant them in the ground. They dropped onto the stretcher with a graceless tumble, the same motion Bud's body made as it toppled into the cool earth to take their place.

Hauling the stretcher of hooch to the boat she wondered what it felt like to lug a wounded man through mud, picking your way through exploding shells and rotting flesh. What would be worse, she thought, the sounds or smells or sights? She decided the worst must be trying to snatch the wounded from a foul and unmarked grave. The other night, as they had heaved and pulled the rumline up from the river shallows, the sweat on Rolly's brow had not been from the warm night. "Thank God, Jonesie," he had said as the first sack from the rumline thudded into the boat. "I had it in my head that we'd lost you in the mud at Canal du Nord after the deserter gave you one in the back." The false peace that had settled over him had also given her a temporary relief.

Now, with Bud gone, they might find a more lasting peace. Emily certainly felt a calmness after she turned the Fair Lady's engine over on one try. She had the touch Bud lacked. There was no way he could have started the boat in time to get away from the Yankee customs men. She'd always suspected he had tipped off the Yanks so they arrived when Joe was down in the shed, leaving Bud to desert her husband in that nearby foreign country. She hoped she'd made the right choice in letting poor Rolly take revenge. It would be another challenge to get the people from Syracuse to deal with her directly, but she had the goods, and faint heart never won fair lady.

# Dr. Spankie's Car

"If the water gets any lower, we'll see the top of Dr. Spankie's car." Father Spratt lifted his cloth cap and scratched his head as he looked out over the Island's rocky shoreline, bare and grey and forty feet further out than normal. Too little snow this winter had left Lake Ontario smaller and meaner, like everything else during the Depression. "Lowest water we've had since the doctor busted through the ice in '23," said the priest, settling his cap low over his forehead.

Tricky Dicky McDermott was thinking about Dr. Spankie's car, too, as he brought the priest home from the sick call on Mrs. LaRush. The wagon ride from the head of the

Island took them all the way along the north shore and with every foot his old mare Minnie plodded, Tricky thought about how the first car on Wolfe Island went under ten years before on a wild December night. Only Dr. Spankie would head out in a storm like that. Several Island families claimed it was to deliver their baby. The roads were done like dinner and the Doc headed onto the ice, swept clean by a mean wind that started up in Toronto and whistled like a bullet for miles and miles down the big lake. But Dr. Spankie hadn't delivered any babies that night. The black Ford cracked through the ice and almost took the doc down with it, but the big man heaved himself through the window just in the nick, then tramped three miles through the snow to the nearest farmhouse. Several Island families claimed he warmed up by their homestead's woodstove. By the time anyone looked out the next morning, the lake was dusted over with snow like a prairie field and there was neither hide nor hair of the Doctor's car.

"That old Ford has put more miles on underwater than on land," said Father Spratt. He was pretty cheery considering he had just given a woman last rites, but Tricky always found Father Spratt a tad cheery for a priest. "People swear they spotted the roof sticking out at the foot of the island," Father said, "or saw a fender down to the head, or a tire in front of the village. Once it even got all the way 'round back to the ridge."

Tricky had a good idea where the old Ford sat. No one knew the winter lake better than him. It was his bread and butter. He had spent years shoving planks over the slushy spots to make toll bridges on the snow road across the ice, charging a nickel to Islanders crossing into town and ten cents to mainlanders coming the other way. He knew all the weak spots and, with the water down and Dr. Spankie in hospital in Kingston breathing out his last, Tricky had been keeping an eye on the most likely location of the old car. Too bad Father Spratt was keeping an eye on Tricky. The priest knew how to keep Island business on the Island but he was a God man and, Island code or no, a God man had his limits. If the wrong folks got to Dr. Spankie's car, then Tricky's ten-year wait for low water would have been for nothing.

The horse turned into the laneway by the big stone church, solid on the foundation Tricky's father had hauled loads of rock and sand for, and they rolled past the stained-glass windows that were the most expensive things on the Island. Down the back lane into the rectory the air was heavy with the lilacs that had burst out and Father Spratt took a deep breath. "Smells like spring," he said.

Tricky helped Father down with the big valise, the one kept by the door with the sick oils in it ready to go, and Father slipped him the usual two bits. Father asked Tricky in for a cup of joe, but time was money and the priest's coffee was no hell anyway. Tricky hopped back up on the seat, slapped the lines against Minnie's rump and they plodded out the laneway, turning the corner towards the

Hitchcock House, which sat smack on the water within spitting distance of the church steps.

The university men were waiting outside the big frame building. Too important to loaf on the veranda, they stood in front with the shovels and picks they tossed into the wagon before Minnie came all the way to a stop. Tricky stayed put on the seat and rolled a smoke.

"What's that contraption?" Tricky was all innocence as he nodded at the metal detector the biggest lad was carefully lifting into the wagon bed.

"It tells us what's under the ground, helps us find artefacts and arrowheads," said the professor, a squirt of a fellow crawling up next to Tricky while his boys piled into the back with the digging gear. The professor must consider Tricky dumb enough to think old arrowheads were made of metal. But Tricky had a pretty good idea what the professor was really looking for and he let the squirt know it on the drive out the road he had just fetched the priest along.

"Funny you looking for an Indian burial ground up the Bateau Channel." Tricky gave Minnie her head since she knew the road better than he did. "Most people look at the other end of the Island, up to Brophy's Point."

"That site is exhausted," said the professor, who had a face like a lady's lap dog. "We have some new and promising indications of native settlement along the old Channel land."

"No one has seen an Indian on the Island in a long, long time," Tricky went on, taking a deep breath of smoke and

44

pausing before he dropped his little bomb. "Not since the French left."

"I am aware of that," said the professor, squirming on the seat when Tricky mentioned the Frenchmen.

"Here's a funny thing," said Tricky. "The old-timers tell about a Frenchman who came ashore right around where you are digging."

"You don't say," said the professor and looked out over the lake, fidgeting with the leather book on his lap. Tricky knew he had the squirt then because he had yet to meet a university man who didn't want to hear the old stories, like his listening was doing you some big favour, like he was telling you the stories were important, as if you didn't know. As if Tricky was too thick to figure out that with Dr. Spankie in the hospital, and the doc an important man, warden for the county and a Member of Parliament, people were looking through his papers and someone in town must have found out the old story about the treasure.

"It was a Frenchman coming across with a sack of gold for LaSalle's camp," Tricky said. "To buy goods and food and pay the men and such. The old-timers say he crossed at Cape Vincent and landed here, burying his gold on the shore and then heading off to find someone to sneak him and his treasure to the fort."

The professor pretended he was reading his big book and not listening to Tricky as they passed the old French castle, burned to the ground a few years back.

"That Frenchman clean disappeared," said Tricky. "Maybe he took off with the gold. Maybe the British got him, or maybe the Indians. Maybe that gold is still sitting out there in the ground."

Tricky waved to the Mac brothers, the whole half-dozen of them picking stones out of the castle field and thumping them onto a stone boat. The Mac brothers straightened up like soldiers and waved back, not a one put his hand to his back even though they had been stooping over rocks before the professor crawled out of the feather tick at the Hitchcock House. The Macs were known for their strong backs, and for being tough as nails and wild as bears. Old Sandy Mac had always hoped a hard day's labour would tire his boys out and when they were young lads he had them pick stones from that field every Saturday in the spring, sun-up to last light. It was steady work; every winter the ice and snow stuck frost fingers deep into the island and pulled up a fresh crop of stones to be cleared out before the plow blades got bent. Sandy Mac was ten years under the soil himself now, the Spanish flu had took him fast, and the boys were men, still picking stone and dumping it along the wood rail fences that divided their smaller and smaller farm lots. Their great-grandfather had been a hard, canny man who had gone from clearing a lone lot with a single axe to owning half of the Island's best farm land. But there was only so much Island to go around, and the Old Mac's ten farming sons had more farming sons and the property had split down and down over the generations, so Sandy Mac's sons were no better off these days than Tricky. They worked together though, and they worked hard. Tricky worked hard, too, but he liked to make more money than some Islanders thought his work worth.

Tricky could still hear the stones dropping onto the stone boat as he touched the lines and Minnie pulled up and the professor and his boys jumped out. Minnie knew as soon as the professor handed over the extra two dollars Tricky charged educated men from town, and she started up back towards the village while the professor and his men began turning over rocks and sniffing like dogs with that metal detector. All that education, thought Tricky, and they're picking stones like the Mac brothers. And all for nothing, if he was right about what was in Dr. Spankie's car.

Because Dr. Spankie had been at Sandy Mac's on that snowy night when his car went through the ice, and Sandy Mac was taking care of his final bit of business, which was a sack that had come up with the stones in the field that year. None of the boys knew what was in it but their hard-as-nails father had turned white as a ghost at the sight of it and took the sack right back to the house and put it under the bed for safe-keeping. There it sat inside an old feed bag until the flu came. Then Sandy Mac called for Dr. Spankie, an educated man, the sort of man who would know what old French coins were worth and how to keep that money on the Island and how to split it among six sons without those bastards in the government finding out. Tricky figured the coins were still in the car or the

47

boys wouldn't be picking stone in that poor field. Tonight he intended to find out, when the rest of the Island was at Mosier's dance hall and a man could slip out on the lake and go about his business without the whole south shore watching.

There was only a fingernail moon when Tricky rowed the skiff out and tossed the rusty chain with the broken prop into the water about a mile off the tip of the Flat Rocks picnic spot. It was slow work dragging the bottom when you were rowing but he didn't want anyone to hear an engine prowling back and forth as he felt around for Dr. Spankie's car. The sound of the band easily covered up his oars and he could hear Art McKenna's fiddle calling Bonaparte's Retreat. The music rolled louder out of the dance hall every time the door opened and the men went out to check the horses and have a sip of rye. Tricky heard the songs change a few times, a reel and a waltz and then a reel again. The tune had changed again, to a low sad song, when he caught something not too far below. Sure enough, he leant over the side and in the light of the muffled lantern he saw the roof of Dr. Spankie's old Ford.

Tricky tugged the prop so it caught hard against the bottom of the car and anchored the skiff, then with special care he tied a rope around his waist. People always seemed surprised that Islanders couldn't swim. An Islander travelled the lake when it was frozen and thawed, in storms and in calm, and took bass and pickerel and muskies out of it to put on the table. Islanders respected the lake for the big thing it was and they didn't splash around in it like a bathtub the way summer people did. Tricky respected the cold spring water, too, when he stepped over the side of the boat. The freezing lake was like a knife on his calves as he stood on the roof of the old Ford, rusty but still rock-hard, by God it was a solid old car. Tricky slipped to his knees and felt under the cold water. He could feel the open window Dr. Spankie had heaved himself out. Tricky didn't much like the idea of heaving himself inside it, but he was thin while Dr. Spankie had been quite a size. He took a deep breath and swung himself over the edge of the car and under the water.

The cold hit his head like a hammer, the chill going all the way to his back teeth. He was blind in the dark night water, too, and gripped the edge of the window tight with his left hand as he felt around inside with the right. He didn't feel anything but what was left of the steering wheel and the slime and muck along the big bench seat, and he had to haul himself back up to the top of the water for another deep breath.

The next time he pulled his top half through the window, his stomach hanging over the door, his legs dangling outside. Holding onto the steering column he pushed himself forward, feeling around in the cold dark with a hand that was going numb. He pulled himself further into the passenger's side, his knees staying just outside, and there he felt it, the right size and shape, where Dr. Spankie had left it ten years before. Tricky grabbed the handle of the doctor's old leather medical bag, slippery and sodden but still in one piece, and wriggled back through the window. The bag moved sluggish in the cold water, like a catfish coming through mud, and it stuck at the window frame. Tricky was losing his breath and he pulled hard, tugging with both hands, and when the bag came rushing through it moved too fast. The handle burst off in his hand and the bag went past him in the blind water, already sinking down towards the bottom.

There was no time for another breath. Tricky loosened the rope and slipped it over his arms and then his head, kicking out from the car and hoping like hell he would find a way back to the top. He waved his arms and thrashed his feet and if he hadn't been so damn wet and cold he would have cried for joy when he bumped up against the bag. He wrapped both arms around it, somehow got his feet on the bottom and gave a mighty jump which brought him to the surface. He could see the dim light of his lantern in the boat a good ten feet away and he let one arm free of the bag and started to splash with it, but there was nothing to grab onto and he felt himself going down, like the water was air that couldn't hold him up.

This time he couldn't find his feet on the bottom, and he couldn't find the car, couldn't find anything to climb on top of, wasn't even sure which way he was facing. He twisted around in the water, holding the bag with both hands, panicking when he felt the weed wrap around him, the long, slippery, leech-ridden strings called seaweed even though this was a lake and not the sea, because Tricky had never seen the sea in his life.

Tricky was not a church-going man but he knew when a prayer was in order. He recalled the rosary his mother made the family say every night before bed, which they kept saying five years after she passed on, till father passed too. It was funny how you never forgot the words, although when he said Holy Mother he was thinking of his own mother, not the Virgin Mary. Tricky's lungs were almost gone, like Sandy Mac's had gone – they said he drowned in his own fluid – and the water still seemed freezing but different, too, like a cold wet blanket closing around him and pulling him down. Then Tricky remembered it was still spring, too early and cold for the weeds that the sun brought up from the bottom of the lake. It was not a weed, it was his own rope, and instead of fighting it he grasped it with his right hand, and hauled himself up and into the boat, somehow still clutching Dr. Spankie's old bag.

He lay there gasping on the bottom of the boat, like the fish he had hauled into it so many times, and it seemed even colder in the night air than in the water. But he reminded himself that he would warm up rowing, that he was not a man for hysterics. He sat himself to the oars and was feeling fine by the time he pulled the boat up on the shore. The Island never looked so good. McKenna's band was playing the Maple Leaf Rag, Minnie was standing right where he left her, and on the seat of the wagon sat

Father Spratt, the one man on the Island who didn't dance any more, putting his black rosary back into his pocket.

"I recall the night Dr. Spankie's car went down as if it was yesterday," said Father, as if they had never stopped their talk on the road. "There are times you need a doctor and times you need a priest. That night Sandy Mac needed a priest and a doctor."

"You have no right to what's in this bag," said Tricky. "I know the law and the law says finders, keepers."

"No man has a right to what's in that bag," said Father Spratt in his priest voice, none too cheery now. "Open it up and we'll see."

Tricky didn't like the sound of that. It was a rare bird who put one over on Tricky Dicky McDermott, but if anybody could it would be this blamed priest. The priest still wasn't smiling when Tricky set the bag down in the wagon bed and used his knife to cut open the clasp at the top. Just like Tricky thought, there were no medicine things inside, no bandages and oils and metal instruments. Just an old feed sack, rotting out and wet. There was no gold, just the chalk white bones of a man, a smashed-in crack in the washed-out skull, like a pickaxe had come down on the forehead.

"That Frenchman has been waiting a long time to lie in a proper churchyard," said Father Spratt, putting the skull back into the bag as if it were a soft and precious metal. "We'll bury him like old Sandy Mac wanted, without putting his family in the professor's history books. We can keep it on the Island, for this old fellow must be part of the

52

Island by now, coming all the way from France with the old families and staying here all this time."

Then Tricky knew where the gold was, that it had once bought half the Island at a shilling per acre, that it was now inside those hard-working men who hauled the stone out of the soil every year. It was so deep into the Island even the hardest frost would never bring it up.

# A Jury Of Her Peers

"They say you've set women back fifty years." The young Toronto Daily Star reporter's voice sounded brutal, even to his own ears, as it rang through a courtroom empty in the wake of the verdict.

"Mr. Hemingway, you flatter me!" cried the flapper delightedly. "To think a giddy thing like me has that kind of sway."

Ernest Hemingway looked over the giddy thing that was Case Doyle. He knew she was about his own age, 24, yet she seemed younger. He had been to war, had married a mature woman, had done some things that made him a man. Case had lived her short pretty life in this Ontario backwater, a place so stolid as to point out with pride that its buildings were a proper, sober slate grey. Still, something was not quite proper, not quite sober, in this giddy thing with the gold-brown eyes.

"The eyes of the country are on you, Miss Doyle," Hemingway said in a gentler voice. "As the first woman in Ontario to serve on a jury, and for a capital crime at that, my editor counts you among the biggest news of 1923."

Not big enough for a reporter of my rank, Hemingway added to himself. This was a story for a cub reporter. Hell, any woman's page editor could do it, but he was being taken down a peg with the "Hindmarsh treatment." He had been the Star's man in Paris when the newsroom pecking order changed. Newspaper politics had seemed far away as he covered the bullfights in Seville and Carpentier's fight and the bobsled run above Chamby. But Hadley wanted to have the baby in North America and now he was in Toronto at the mercy of Harry Hindmarsh, the assistant managing editor who had married the owner's daughter and who thought writing anything but "a punch in every paragraph" was an ugly pretension.

"What a scream," Case laughed. "Hart Myers was just the sort to think his passing deserved the sighs of thousands and you've been sent all the way from Toronto to see if I would hang the woman supposed to have killed him."

The travel was a sore point. Hemingway had paid top dollar for a last-minute seat on the train to this self-important town north of Lake Ontario and south of nowhere. He would soon be a family man, with responsibilities, and he kept a close account of expenses. Not that he wasn't glad to get out of Hogtown, as they aptly called that pig-ugly burg. If one more of its uncouth citizens suggested he trade his beret for a fedora, or told him to put on a tie or get a shine, he would bust. But Hogtown was home, for his sins, and if he wrapped this up fast he could catch the five o'clock flyer back to Hadley.

"How did you come to your verdict?" he said. Case was the last woman Hemingway would have trusted to discern a murderer's guilt. She looked like a kitten in a crate as she stretched across the front row seat in the otherwise empty jury box. Her bobbed hair looked soft and shiny, her raised eyebrows were unplucked and blonde, and she had not concealed the unfashionable freckles sprinkled across her nose. Her mink stole, a bit much given the mild fall weather and her role as a juror, was draped casually over the thick mahogany rail that separated twelve good people from the court. Only her wicked jaw, which set with determination at the spectators' collective gasp over the verdict, suggested character.

"I put it down to the lemonade," she chattered on. "Dollar Bill sells the loveliest lemonade, he puts just the teensiest kick in it. The night Aggie Harder was arrested I was on my fourth lemonade when Dicky Cunningham came in looking like he'd been through the mill – you saw Dicky, he's the Crown Attorney, didn't he give a cracker-jack show today? – Dicky didn't want to dish at first, Hart Myers was a pal from the RAF, but it was the talk of the town and, really, we are usually such a quiet town, Mr. Hemingway."

"It's a swell town," he said. It was barely a mile from one end to the other and jammed with sombre limestone monuments, the City Hall once intended as the country's capital building, the Anglican and Catholic cathedrals, the Masonic Lodge, the Customs House, not to mention the well-kept shops of the butcher, the grocer, the tobacconist. At first glance the decadence supposed to have descended on the world since the end of the War and the start of Prohibition seemed to be passing the city by.

"Most of the time we're pretty ho-hum, nothing but high teas and afternoon at homes," Case sighed. "But the Americans have that silly rule about not distilling liquor, whereas our government thinks it a sin to let a profitable distillery sit idle, even if the citizens aren't supposed to indulge. Things get very silly when the Americans arrive for the summer, with the distillery working overtime and the speakeasies along the river filled with women bathing in bathtubs of gin and masked college men running hounds and hares. But it's all so harmless, and Hart's murder had us topsy-turvy. Even Dicky was acting screwy, although we finally got him to admit Aggie had shimmied down the tree outside her room on the night of the murder. Escaping the paternal despot, we thought, for the dashing lover waiting to whisk her away across the border."

Hemingway thought of the thick-soled night watchman from the Davis Tannery, blinking gravely like an owl in the sunlight as he testified he had seen the accused climbing out of her bedroom window. Yes, he had the right house, didn't everyone know the Harders' house, didn't banker Thomas Harder have the biggest house on King Street and didn't the watchman pass it at the same time every night?

"It was so romantic, like something out of the moving pictures," Case sighed.

It didn't sound romantic in court, Hemingway thought. It sounded cheap. The stoop-shouldered Harder père had huddled miserably amid the courtroom spectators as the watchman described how the defendant leapt from the lowest bough and drew up her black cloak with both hands, running off with all possible speed to meet her married lover. Here in Canada, Que Nada as he and Hadley called it, appearance was all and the little vamp had already put a permanent stain on the banker's name. In Paris no one would have turned a hair at a fresh young thing so eagerly seeking sex.

The fresh young thing in front of him prattled on. "Dicky said the scuttlebutt would come out in front of a jury of Aggie's peers and I said don't be absurd, how can a woman get a jury of her peers if her peers aren't on the jury? There's no reason women can't be jurors, we've had the vote for five years, for pete's sake. Dicky declared that women were so soft-hearted they could never tell when the wool was being pulled over their eyes. I thought he was talking about Aggie, that he was bitter about how Hart had led her on. Dicky was always sweet on Aggie but too much the respectable married man to do anything about it."

"The Crown was sweet on her?" Hemingway asked. "But he went at her like a tiger."

"He was a positive beast!" She lowered her voice, drew back her slim shoulders, and did a passable impression of the Crown Attorney. " 'Tell me, Miss Harder, as you stumbled in the road, falling in your haste to escape the scene of that loathsome slaying, as you lay in the dirt calling for your mother, did you spare a thought for that other mother, the poor widow with the now orphaned child?' I got a chill down my spine as she sat there a proper lady, white gloves folded in her lap, replying in that clear voice, 'Dicky darling, if I'd thought at all I never would have got myself into this mess.'"

"Well, I could say the same thing about this jury duty, for what a donnybrook Dicky and I had over it at the speak, with me letting fly and claiming I could always tell when Aggie Harder lied. We've been in the bridge club so long I knew she twiddles her pearls 'round her finger when she's bluffing about trump. Only a woman could spot that, I said, and right there and then I bet him a mink coat that the only way Aggie would get a fair trial was if a woman was on the jury."

Hemingway imagined her making the wager, her coquettish rashness, her open amusement, the glint in her tawny eyes as she sized up the man and enjoyed the competition. He was beginning to think she might be a funny and interesting girl to know.

"I had forgotten all about it the next day but Roy Larkin, the city clerk, is a cheeky devil, always takes a joke too far. He got his position because his father is our Member of Parliament and he, Roy, hasn't settled into harness. To top it off the chucklehead is still sore I wouldn't accompany him to the spring ball. He thought it a great prank to send me that jury duty notice and teach me a lesson in this oh-so-manly courtroom." The silver bangles on her wrist jingled merrily as she gestured dramatically around the masculine temple to justice with its heavy, wooden panels rising two-thirds of the way up the wall and the newish stained-glass windows in memory of the heroes of the Great War.

"He thought I'd be a good girl and watch the menfolk mete out justice and be sorry I ever blew my own bazoo. He thought Larry Kirkpatrick — that's the defense attorney, wasn't he dreamy in his marvelous black robe, so sympathetic, getting Aggie to reveal how she had been intending to do the noble thing and send Hart packing, only to find him lying in a pool of blood, how it was so horrible and traumatizing that she didn't remember what happened next, how she thought she had dreamed the whole thing till the police came pounding on her father's door! – well Roy thought Larry would put the kibosh on it and banish me from the jury box."

"But Kirkpatrick was counting on a woman's sensitive nature."

"He took a chance! Women don't look kindly on a girl who can be seduced with a mink coat and soft words by a New York slick, no offence, Mr. Hemingway."

"I'm from Illinois." Oak Park, he might have said, was no place for slicks. It was a place of narrow minds and broad lawns where any self-respecting Canadian would have felt at home. It had been a while since he lived there and he wondered if he would find a girl as entertaining as Case if he went back.

"We all knew Aggie Harder was trouble waiting to happen," she continued. "Don't get me wrong, Aggie was a saint nursing her mother through that horrible sickness. But when her mother was gone all the serious bits in Aggie were gone, too. Her father has been mad as spit at her ever since, he gave her a terrible trimming when she called it quits with the respectable young sap he wanted her to marry. We didn't see her for a month, not till she figured out how to get down that tree. But you could no more lock Aggie up than lock up a moonbeam. She was the most whizz-bang, thorough-going flapper. She loved a touch of drink and a peppy story and dancing and flirting with married men and talk of travelling to gay places in automobiles and trains and ocean liners and such."

Just a few short months ago Hemingway and Hadley had been telling peppy stories and drinking café crème in the garden at the Stade Anastasie where the boxers waited on tables before rounds in the ring. Their last ride on an ocean liner had seen Hadley retching all the way across a heaving Atlantic, their final destination a fourth-floor, walk-up flat on Bathhurst Street, where the only acceptable recreation was church-going.

"Aggie's a clotheshorse," Case said, "although you couldn't tell by the dreary getup she wore in the dock, that horrible black wool serge with the high collar and her pearls in a respectable double loop. You should have seen her the night she met Hart at Dollar Bill's. She had on an orchid chiffon evening gown covered in rhinestone and crystal embroidery, all flowers and leaves and wild things, and her mother's pearls slung across her chest in the most indecent droop. She looked like a moonbeam, all sparkles and light. She and Dicky were dancing, and laughing at the song. It was 'Yes, We Have No Bananas,' and they kept up the joke when Dicky introduced her to his old pal Hart, who was in town to sell boxes to the distillery. Hart pronounced the song splendid, expression unfettered by the demands of intelligence and as important a contribution to the intellectual life of America as the prose of Gertrude Stein."

"Miss Stein wouldn't like that," Hemingway said with a pang for that substantial woman and her foreign salon filled with Cezanne, Matisse, Picasso, and other nouveau and wicked things, and food and tea and distilled fruit liqueurs in small cut-crystal glasses. "She and I are great friends and I know she has no use for popular music."

"You don't say," said Case. "Hart didn't know Miss Stein at all, it was just the sort of clever thing he said. He was very clever. We all had a pash for him, even after Dicky told us about the wife and the baby and the box factory. Hart's eyes were much like yours, dark and sheikhish, glaring at you and through you, missing nothing and seeing

63

something that might not be there. When Hart gave Aggie that mink coat, the most topping of minks, I was green with envy. She wore it everywhere, no matter how warm the night. I'd have grabbed that coat in a jiffy because I only have this silly stole, which has barely any style at all."

She gave the mink stole a resentful poke and it slithered off the rail. As he stooped to pick it up, Hemingway wondered what Case would look like wearing Hadley's no-longer-new cloth coat, if her vibrant air could be contained in a battered cotton shell. He said, "A mink sets a fellow back a bit."

"They both thought it worth the jack, although if Aggie's pater had caught wind of it, they'd have been quits. But she got so she could shimmy out the window wearing mink, pearls, high heels and all and not even muss her hair. They got on like a house on fire and when the day came for Hart to go back to Ithaca and he didn't, we thought he'd chuck the wife and the box factory. Dicky tried to talk sense into them. A discreet summer fling is one thing but divorce is a terrible scandal. It would have meant the absolute ruin of Aggie. She'd have been disgraced, never able to set foot in decent society again, and you can't spend all your time in speakeasies, can you?"

Hemingway had wondered how a man ran with the bulls in this Presbyterian-soaked country, how a man tested his mettle outside of a boxing ring. Now, looking at this swashbuckling girl in this dull, carping city, he saw a dangerous possibility.

"What swayed you?" he asked. "The fact she didn't touch her pearls?"

"Of course I was watching for the dead giveaway ... pardon the expression! Especially when Dicky went at Aggie hammer and tongs, and she never touched the necklace, not even during that cruel bit about her crying out for her mother."

"Pearls are a thin strand to hang a verdict on."

"Yes, but then of course there's the mink," Case said, in a way that implied the young reporter must know what she meant.

"The mink," repeated Hemingway, in a way he hoped did not reveal he had no idea what she meant.

"She wore it everywhere, so why leave it at home if she was going to run away? She didn't wear the mink because she really was giving Hart the brush and didn't want to hand it over in an honorable gesture. Minks are so much warmer than honorable gestures. And there was the suitcase."

"No one mentioned a suitcase."

"Exactly! A fashion plate like Aggie couldn't make a getaway without a full trousseau, bride or no, but the watchman saw her running with empty hands. No suitcase, no plans to take it on the lam."

Hemingway thought of the trunk, still packed with Hadley's little horde of riches, stuffed into a corner in the Toronto apartment. It held only her treasures, for she had lost his, the Chicago manuscript, the Paris sketches, the long fishing story, all in the crummy valise stolen, she said, at the Gare de Lyon while she was buying Evian water. He said, "Your pal the Crown nixed his own prosecution with a drunken bet."

"Thoroughly sober," Case said. "He knew it was a bum rap."

"Because she didn't touch her necklace or wear a pricey coat?"

"Because he killed Hart Myers, of course! How else could he have known Aggie toppled over when she lit out after finding the body? Or that she called out for her mama? Aggie was so dotty with shock she couldn't say what she did after finding Hart, and who could have seen her stumbling about but the killer? Poor Dicky, prosecuting an innocent woman, one he loved enough to kill for, but unable to confess without ruining the good name of his lawful wife and kiddies. No wonder he wanted me on that jury."

"He knew you'd hang it."

"What else could I do? We may seem small and backwards here but we know what's what. Perhaps you can't grasp it, the idea of a decent enough fellow who wants something so impossible and so perfect and so foolish that he can't stand by and see it spoiled forever by a careless heart. But this is just a story to you, Mr. Hemingway, you just want to write it up and get back to your life."

Hemingway did grasp it. But it was a damn good story, too, and it would show Hindmarsh a thing or two about getting a scoop. These new developments were worth making this an overnight trip, and he said so, adding "If I print this, your pal will be arrested and you won't collect that mink coat he wagered."

"Well, there must be easier ways to earn a mink," sighed Case. "Any ideas, Mr. Hemingway?"

# A Christmas Bauble

**Dan Tuttle would not** have spent Christmas Eve with a shotgun pointed at his head if the woman he adored did her gift shopping on time. But asking Case Doyle to do her shopping on time – to do anything on time – was asking for a Christmas miracle.

Case was a perfect specimen of what the Saturday magazines called a flapper and she stood out in December-grey Kingston like a rose on a casket. Her hair and her skirts were too short, her laugh too full. She danced even when her feet weren't moving and she wanted flying lesson for Christmas. She liked aeroplanes, gin, masked parties, the Charleston and, apparently, Elliot "Sammy"

69

Sampsen, the too-charming son of a director of the railway. By all rights it should have been the well-bred Sammy staring down the shotgun barrel. But, if Dan had learned anything in the Great War, it was that the Dans of this world stared down the barrel while the Sammys had Christmas brunch with pretty, laughing girls.

Case laughed as she and Dan dashed out the front door of the newspaper office where they worked, although with Case "work" was a word to be used loosely. It had been snowing since before dawn and King Street was blanketed a foot thick. Dan would never have guessed a weapon existed in this clean, white city. It was five years since the Armistice and he still thought of death as muddy and wet and reeking.

"Bright and crisp and even," Case sang, hugging herself inside the mink coat she had won in a bet with a Toronto reporter.

This was the scene Dan dreamed of in the trenches, when he realized he would not be home for Christmas after all. Horses and sleighs slid past, harnesses jingling, tree branches were iced with snowdrops, passers-by called out cheery greetings, all modern machines banished by the snow. Even Case, who loved to drive and went everywhere in top gear, left her rich aunt's car buried in the snow and skipped along in silly red leather boots like the ones Greta Garbo sported in a picture at the Bijou. When Dan asked how Case knew they were red, given that the movie had no colour, she accused him of lacking imagination. Dan had lots of imagination, and Case played a big

70

role in his imagining, but it never seemed the time to tell her.

As they turned the corner to plunge through the drifts along Princess Street, snow beaded the lenses of Dan's glasses, making it hard to see. Case got a few steps ahead despite the slippery soles of her fancy boots. "You should've shopped earlier," Dan called, thinking of his gift for her, tucked in his coat pocket.

"Danny, I had no idea working was going to take up so much time," Case said over her shoulder. "Anyway, I didn't have a cent for Aunt Stella's present until I cornered Colonel Smiley in the business office and got advanced a month's pay."

A month's pay! Eighty dollars! For a Christmas present! Dan's gift seemed smaller now. But Case did not have annoying inconveniences like room and board and the occasional clean shirt. She lived with her aunt, the newspaper's publisher, in a big house far from the breweries and locomotive works and factories stretching across the busy Kingston harbour. The smell of tanning hides and belching engines did not wake Aunt Stella – Mrs. Matthews to Dan and the ordinary joes at the newspaper – from her feather bed. Case literally breathed a different air, one that made her want to fly and gave her breath to loudly nickname the bully who ran the newspaper's business office. "Colonel Smiley," as Case dubbed him, was the perfect officer; short, scheming and charming. He had been spending an awful lot of the time lately with the widowed Aunt Stella, and Dan had not confronted him about the weekly pay

71

packet regularly coming up a dollar light. If there was one thing Dan learned in the trenches, it was to keep his head down.

"Charge! Into the breach!" Case shouted. Marten van Strien was putting the closed sign in the door of his jewellery store and Case flung herself over the threshold, sending the jeweller staggering. Dan hurled himself behind Case because, well, because he couldn't help himself, and they landed in a heap on the carpeted floor. Dan's glasses fogged up as he collapsed on Case's soft mink and he could smell her perfume, like no flower he had ever smelled, light and foreign and expensive.

Dan got to his feet, heard the door shut and the lock click, and wondered why Case had not yet made a smart remark. He pulled off mittens crusted with sharp snow and rubbed his glasses on a speck of wool that seemed dry. The lenses were streaky when he put them on and he thought he wasn't seeing right. He took off the glasses, rubbed harder, and pushed them firmly back up his nose – but he was still staring down the barrel of a shotgun held by a woman very, very great with child.

"Kitty Beaupre!" he said.

"Dan Tuttle, still following Case Doyle like a lapdog," said Kitty. The butt of the shotgun was resting against her huge belly, clearly she did not know about its kick. She was a tiny thing with a sharp tongue, snapping eyes and a proud, thin face with faint pink trails of acne. Dan had always liked her even though she was the most expert lip-curler-upper he had ever met. She sometimes filled in as a bookkeeper at the newspaper, scrounging work she had done full-time when the men were away at war. She was as alone in the world as Dan – and she was not married, as her naked ring finger proclaimed.

"I've heard of shotgun weddings," Case said, her nose out of joint from the lapdog comment. "But this is a crackerjack idea. Steal a ring, capture a bachelor like Dan, and wait for a minister to come by."

Shut up, Dan thought, wondering if he had lived through Passchendaele to be shot by a deceived woman.

"Shut up," said Kitty. Her swollen body seemed to fill the narrow shop made small by thick glass display shelves running along walls darkened by wood-panelling and red velvet wallpaper. Dan felt as if he were trapped inside a leaded glass snow globe, like the one his mother brought out every Christmas until the Spanish flu took her.

"Can't wait for Christmas morning, can you Case?" Kitty said bitterly.

"No, I can't," said Case, getting to her feet in a wet swirl of leather and mink. "But that's not a shooting offence."

"If you are going to rob me, Kitty, get done with it," said Marten van Strien in his dry, accented voice. The tall, unbending Dutchman was a man of few words and not because he was ashamed of pronouncing his w's as v's and j's as y's. During the War some Kingston businessmen had changed their foreign-sounding names but van Strien stubbornly kept his, and his business, too. Everyone knew the Dutch knew diamonds and no one wanted a bad diamond, so in the end everyone bought from van Strien because of his foreign name. Even Dan had bought a trinket from the jeweller's shop.

"Who says I'm robbing you?" asked Kitty. "I don't want your lousy jewels."

"Are you sure?" asked Case. "A nice bauble is right up there with flying lessons on today's Christmas gift list."

Enough with the flying, thought Dan. Get your feet on the ground.

"Why would I want a nice bauble?" spat Kitty. "To remind me of the heel who left me broke and in trouble while he bought another woman a flashy jewel for Christmas?"

"You have a point," said Case thoughtfully. "That's the work of a Grade A rat."

"You bet he's a rat," said Kitty. "Living it up while I hide away, trying not to starve to death. When I found out he was getting his lady friend a Christmas bauble, I decided to give him my own two-barrelled present."

"Shooting does sound too good for the hound," said Case. "But the majority of folks will say hanging is too good for you and that doesn't sound good at all."

Kitty smiled a grim smile and tightened her grip on the barrel. "Easy for you to say, with a big rock coming straight to your ladylike finger on Christmas morning."

"A big rock?" said Case with too much interest, and Dan felt what was left of his heart sink into his stomach. "How big?"

"The biggest," snarled Kitty. "Show her." She nodded curtly towards the jeweller, expecting to be obeyed, and Dan thought she would have made a good sergeant. Van Strien took an engraved silver casket from one of the glass displays and handed it to Case, who expertly flipped it open. Nesting haughtily on the purple velvet was the biggest ring Dan had ever seen, and his own gift for Case shrank to nothing at all.

"Diamonds and platinum on rose gold," said Case. "One wonders if this a Christmas bauble or a serious proposition." She slipped the ring on her finger and extended her hand to see the stone sparkle.

"It's our finest engagement ring," said van Strien.

And a too-serious proposition, Dan thought miserably. Case would wear Sammy's ring and be married in June by the bishop in the cathedral. They would go on a summer honeymoon to the Continent and come home to a big house on the lake. She would never work at the newspaper again and Dan would sometimes glimpse her driving by, too fast, in a big motor car. Sammy would be his new boss, and Sammy and the Colonel would be thick as thieves. Dan wondered if The British Whig was looking for reporters, or maybe The Intelligencer in Belleville.

RAP-RAP-RAP. The sharp, sudden sound sent Dan diving to the floor before he realized he was moving, slave to a reaction he thought long dead. He cursed himself when he realized it had been a knock on the door, and a sharp voice Dan despised called out, "Let me in."

"By all means, let His Nibs in," Kitty ordered. Van Strien opened the door and Colonel Smiley strolled in, took off his expensive fedora, and shook snow from the brim onto the jeweller's carpet in front of Dan's prone body.

"Kitty Beaupre, what do you think you are doing?" barked the Colonel in his command voice.

"Wiping the smile off your mug for good," Kitty snarled, shoving the barrel of the shotgun against the little man's chest. "You two-timing louse."

"Darling Kitty," purred the colonel, suddenly turning an 100-watt electric smile on his small, handsome face. "You misjudge me. You're the only girl for me."

"Lay off the soft soap," she said. "I've had enough of your darling Kitty's and opening doors and driving me home as if I were sugar that might melt in the rain."

"Now Kitty," said the Colonel, with a look of gentle rebuke Dan thought he must have practised in a mirror. "Is that any way to talk to the man who has come to buy you a special Christmas gift?"

"My gift?" Kitty said. "It's for the rich widow you've been chasing."

Kitty was talking tough but Dan could see she wanted to believe, because it must look like her problems would be over if he gave her child his name. Dan, though, figured her problems would be just beginning if she married that skunk.

"It's the season for putting things right," the Colonel pleaded. "Show me some good will, darling Kitty."

"You were dipping into the accounts," Kitty said softly. "Shaving a little off where you thought people wouldn't complain. You only made time with me when I found out about it."

"Kitty, you've got it all wrong," said the Colonel. "The money was for us, for our family."

"He's a liar and a thief," said Case quietly. "He hoped no one would believe a woman in your, er, delicate condition."

"Of course you'd say that," snapped Kitty. "It was your money he stole and your aunt he's trifled with. It would kill the likes of you to admit he might prefer the likes of me."

"And I do, Kitty," said the Colonel, slowly opening his arms wide. "Indeed, I do."

Kitty lowered the gun and stepped into the Colonel's embrace. He hugged her, stepped back and gently took the shotgun from her hands. Then he slapped her across the face, slamming her into the display case. Dan heard Case's sharp gasp as Kitty fell to the carpet, broken glass and engagement rings spilling about her, her huge stomach straining against her thin cloth coat.

"You ridiculous tramp," said the Colonel calmly, breaching the gun and ejecting the shells as if he had just finished a pheasant shoot. "That brat could be anyone's."

Van Strien squatted beside Kitty, Dan thought to pick up his spilled jewellery. But the jeweller took off his jacket and folded it into a pillow for Kitty's head. Then he tenderly began to pick the broken glass from Kitty's hair, saying, "There, there." Kitty began to cry and Dan wanted to cry, too, seeing that proud woman in tears at such a little act of kindness.

That was when Dan felt things slow down, like when he was about to scramble out of that trench. As he got to his feet he felt his left foot travel forward in a long falling step. His weight shifted, his half-opened left hand coming straight out from his shoulder, chin high, and his fingers began to close with a mad clutch, his knuckles lining up like soldiers, and he hit Colonel Smiley, hard, square in his smooth, smug face. Smiley hit the carpet like a ton of bricks, the same bricks which seemed to have fallen from Dan's shoulders, and lay still. Dan was leaning over, ready to throttle the Colonel, when Kitty screamed an unearthly shriek and clutched her distended stomach.

"We must get to the hospital," van Strien said. "Now."

"Carry on without me," Case said, poking the still-out Kaiser with a red-booted toe. "I have a Christmas present to take care of."

How selfish, Dan thought, as he gathered the pregnant woman into his arms, for Case to be thinking of her own Christmas at a time like this. It made him as sad as anything he had seen in Flanders.

"Do all babies look like Queen Victoria?" Case was saying when Dan dropped by the hospital the next morning.

"My baby looks like an angel," the new mother said with her old spunk. She was sitting up in bed and putting the infant to her breast and Dan, about to walk into the room, blushed and stepped back.

"I'm sure she's a fine specimen," Case said, "as far as babies go. In fact, I'd say your Christmas angel deserves a present."

Dan peeped through the crack between the door and the frame and saw her presenting Kitty with the envelop full of the month's pay. "Think of it as a belated wedding gift," she said.

"Very funny," Kitty sniffed.

"I am as serious as the heart attack I am wishing on the now unemployed Colonel Smiley," Case said, handing over a newspaper. "I was going over a back issue of the Chronicle and realized I missed your wedding announcement in February. How romantic, you marrying your young pilot on Valentine's Day."

"My young pilot?" said Kitty, peering at the page in one hand, cradling the child with the other.

"It's right there in black and white, suitable for framing," said Case vaguely, and Dan wondered what strings she pulled to have the notice printed up.

"How sad to think you were married to the dashing young fly-boy in February and a widow by August," Case went on, giving Kitty another sheet of newsprint. "A young man crashing in the prime of life – see it says right here, 'the prime of life.' And while out barn-storming a living for his wife and coming child. It's heartbreaking."

"Heart-breaking," echoed Kitty, her eyes tearing across the page.

"But not as sad as the story in tomorrow's paper, about the poor widow trying to sell her engagement ring on Christmas Eve. Mr. van Strien gave such a lovely quote. 'A woman's engagement ring ought to be sacred.' Mr. van Strien is a secret romantic, the stiff old stick. That reminds me, you left your ring behind and your gold band, too." And Case handed over the little silver casket with Sammy's ring.

"But Sammy –," Kitty began.

"Won't be needing a ring," interrupted Case. "I adore the stylish way he swans about with his hands in his pockets and he's a wonder with a martini shaker. But the future Mrs. Sammy is in for a lifetime of bridge parties, collecting china dogs and long stories about men named Binky Batson. A girl doesn't want to spend her life with the wrong fellow just because the hoi polloi demand it."

Dan had heard people say their hearts soared but he had never understood what they meant. Now he heard trumpets sound, angels sing, and all was right in the heavens. Case had helped Kitty when no one else could, she didn't love that silly man, and she was a pretty, laughing girl who wanted to fly. Dan coughed loudly, gave Kitty time to settle the baby, and strolled into the room with his hands in his pockets.

"I brought you a present, Kitty," he said, handing over the gift he had bought for Case. Kitty unwrapped it carefully, saving the tissue paper and the little cardboard box, and drew out the tiny airplane suspended on a silver chain.

"Dan, that is the most beautiful Christmas bauble I have ever seen," breathed Case.

"A belated wedding gift," he smiled, "in memory of Kitty's pilot."

Kitty was wearing the necklace when she and her baby drifted off to sleep and the nurse came in to give Case and Dan the push.

"Why don't you come back to the old homestead for Christmas brunch?" Case said, taking Dan's hand, puffy and red from bashing the Colonel. "There are all the essentials for a jolly time, spiked punch and fruitcake and mistletoe and the like."

He could smell her French cologne as she leaned in to kiss him on the cheek and for the first time he knew what it felt like to be a hero.

# Trifling Matters

**When I first asked people** to pay to speak to the dead, I didn't expect them to treat a séance like a haircut. It reminds me of a clown I saw in a play (All's Well That Ends Well on the West End in the last year of the Great War and quite funny, all things considered.) "A barber's chair fits all buttocks," the clown said, then described a lot of asses.

Five years later and half a world away, I think of that clown every time I peek at the guests in my waiting room in this grey Canadian city. Some want to be transformed, some to keep a look they should outgrow. They all want their money's worth.

Last night I peered from behind the curtain to see Willie had arrived early, as usual, and sat reading his newspaper. The headlines announced Death had visited and a girl from a good family was found dead behind the British American Hotel, but Willie folded over the page to a story about the new tax proposed for thoroughbred racetracks. (I'll never get used to the Canadian love of "sin tax." Who else would pass Prohibition laws that keep distilleries open so they can be taxed, yet forbid the sale of liquor to their own people?) Willie would vote on the new tax when it came to Parliament and so must have read the story in the early edition. That meant he hoped to be recognized.

Willie is one of the most famous men in the country but often goes unnoticed because he looks like every dull middle-aged Canadian holding forth in a courtroom or classroom. Medium height, thin hair, shined shoes, fussy in his dress down to the waistcoat with straining buttons and gold watch chain. But he was in luck: The next guest was a military man who came to a dead stop at the sight of him, wondering whether to leave, salute, or both. Willie nodded towards an armchair, looking pleased as he went back to his newspaper.

The military man was a new guest, old enough to have served in France and handsome enough for moving pictures. He reminded me of that French clown, Max Linder, who looked so sad when he returned to Hollywood after the War. He had the same thick, well-trimmed moustache and large, melancholy eyes. He took off his cap and sat, staring at a rather fine painting of my second husband, the lumber baron, until the seven-fingered gambler came in.

Bertie Harpell had been to three séances, paid for one, and received no hot tips (spirits are funny about numbers). He reminded me of my first husband, who never said die until a German ace in a Fokker fighter plane said it for him. There was something Kipling-you-will-be-a-man in the way Bertie held his head and stretched to his full five and a half feet, tucking his damaged hand into his pocket. When Bertie visited, I wondered if my first husband would finally send a message through the veil, but I fancy he was busy drinking single malt and playing cards with Keats and Owen and other dead poets.

Bertie nodded to the other men, took a seat, drew the racing newspaper and a pencil from a pocket, and began jotting notes. The men sat in an amiable triangle of newspaper rattling, pencil scratching, and staring, until the girl strode in.

Young ladies usually come as a gaggle, honking, fluttering, and confusing the spirits so that messages get silly, all handsome strangers, long journeys to romantic places, and children to be born. This girl was what Willie's newspaper called a flapper. Her bobbed hair was shiny, her eyebrows un-plucked, and she had not done a thing about her freckles. She wore an airplane charm on a gold chain. Her mink coat should have looked too old for her, but the red leather boots made it come out right. As she shrugged off the mink, all three men rose to take it. The soldier yielded to Willie, who set down the paper with the tax

85

story facing up, then wiped his hands with a white hand-kerchief. Bertie lagged in the backstretch. Willie put on his best smile. "I'm Willie," he said, drawing out the nickname as if it had the eight syllables by which the public knew him. I doubted someone that young knew who he was. I was wrong.

"Of course, you are," she said. "How terribly exciting. I am sure this raises the bar for tonight's event, affairs of state and all that."

"This is strictly personal, my dear," said Willie, handing her coat to the Captain. "Indeed, I prefer one-on-one con-sultations, but Madame suggested a group session would open more conduits."

(I'd fibbed about the conduits. One must discreetly ad-vertise one's services and letting others see the quality of the clientele brings in bookings.)

"Of course," said girl. "One cannot govern one's coun-try on the advice of the spirits. That would be silly."

"We'll say no more about it," said Willie. "Such a pretty girl must be allowed some latitude." Willie is a great flat-terer. After a one-on-one reading I sometimes feel I've been licked by a purring cat.

"How do you do," the girl turned to the soldier, her hand outstretched in greeting.

"Captain Jean-Marc St. Pierre," said the soldier. He took her fingers, elegantly turned her wrist and dipped his handsome head to kiss her hand. "*Enchanté mademoi-selle.*"

"*Je m'appelle* Case Doyle," said the girl. "*J'adore tout chose français.* I'm sure it will bring an extra *frisson* to tonight's events as we *parley-vous* with the spirits. Are you here to speak to anyone in particular?"

The Captain smiled. "I am here because I lost a bet. But now, mademoiselle, I do not feel so unlucky."

"I won my mink in a bet, *quelle coïncidence, n'est-ce pas*?" said Case. "Wagers have the most interesting outcomes."

"I have always thought so," said the gambler, grasping her fingers with his good hand in a hail-fellow-well-met grip. "Do call me Bertie."

"Bertie, I would be delighted," said the girl, looking up at him. (I had thought her taller when she came in.) "You must call me Case."

"Always a pleasure to meet a fellow speculator," said Bertie.

"My friend Hattie was the real gambler," said Case. "Always off to the races with her secret lover. The last place you'd find her parents was playing the ponies, so they never caught her canoodling by the rail."

"I am delighted to hear someone had luck trackside," said Bertie.

"For a while," said Case. "Hattie picked horses with charming names and the secret lover placed the bets. Très Chic came in at 20-1 and paid for the golden charm he bought her when he promised to leave his wife – the wife being the reason he was the secret lover. They were going to fly off somewhere impossibly romantic."

"I like stories about winners," said Bertie.

"Sadly, her luck did not hold," said Case.

"It never does," said Bertie.

"It's Hattie I want to contact," said Case. "Hers was a sudden departure with no exit lines. So here I am for my first séance."

"An interesting choice," said the Captain.

"My cousin Artie has a sideline pushing spiritualism," said Case, "and now I have come alive to it — if one might put it that way."

"You are most fortunate in your maiden outing," said Willie. "Madame is unsurpassed. You could not find a safer pair of hands."

"She knows her way around the course," said Bertie. "Keeps tight to the rail."

"I hear she is a marvel," said Case.

Time to make my entrance. I swooshed through the curtain and greeted my guests, making sure to press Willie's hand a little longer than the others, then shepherded them into my darkened salon. It's a well-appointed room crowded with the heavy, brown furniture Canadians love, including some top-drawer pieces left me by the lumber baron. At the centre of the room was a round rosewood table with five matching chairs and a lit beeswax candle.

"What a lovely scent," said the girl.

"Spirits are attracted to the honey aroma. It helps them connect to the physical plane," I said. (The beeswax also drips onto the Irish linen tablecloth and is the devil to wash out.)

"It's so dark," said Case. "How atmospheric."

"Spirits find bright lights disorienting when coming through the veil," I said, drawing shut the waiting room curtain and further darkening the room.

"Like coming out of the London subway and blinking in the light," Case said. "I expect I'll feel the same tonight."

"It will doubtless be an elucidating experience," said Willie.

"I do hope so," said Case. "Cousin Artie says education never ends, it is a series of lessons with the greatest for the last."

"Well put," said Willie. "Is your cousin a teacher?"

"We Doyles earn our crusts by scribbling," said Case. "Cousin Artie had a tremendous go pulling his pen across paper until he lost his son to the Somme and the influenza. Now he's more interested in séancing."

"*C'est tragique*," said St. Pierre. "The world has too many grieving fathers."

"Sadly, you will have too much experience there, Captain," said Case. "Are you afraid of ghosts?"

"*Pas du tout*," said St. Pierre. "There is nothing to fear from the dead."

"We'll see about that," said Case.

"You must not be afraid, my dear," said Willie, patting the chair beside him. "Sit next to me and I shall be your guardian through the night's events."

"I would be honoured," said Case. She would no doubt have preferred the Captain take the chair on her other side, but Bertie slid in and left the Captain to close the circle to my right.

"Will be there be ectoplasm?" Case said. "Cousin Artie says ectoplasm can be messy and this is a new dress."

"It is a lovely frock," said Willie.

"*Très belle*," said the Captain.

"It's a lulu," agreed the girl.

"What's ectoplasm?" said Bertie.

"A physical emanation of spirit essence, a sort of phosphorescent gel, that emerges from the medium," I said. "But do not expect to see it tonight. My channeling is on the auditory plane."

"Will there be tambourines and trumpets?" said the girl. "Cousin Artie once saw a trumpet levitate and play Making Whoopee."

"This is a serious affair, my dear," said Willie, who is good at sounding avuncular. "You should conduct yourself as if at a church service."

"My method is simple," I said, taking my seat. "We join hands to conduct our psychic energy. Then I commune with my spirit guide, who in turn reaches out to other spirits."

"Like a telephone exchange," said the girl. "You're the operator dialing a line."

"Get me St. Peter," said Bertie, "and the inside scoop on the third race at Woodbine."

"I am the medium," I said. "You ask questions through me."

"I love questions," said Case, "almost as much as trumpets."

"*Est-ce dangereux*?" said the Captain. "Perhaps too disturbing for an unescorted young lady, no matter how pretty?"

"It is *beaucoup galant* of you to think so," said Case.

"You are quite safe, my dear," said Willie. "I shall keep a close eye on you."

"Now we call my spirit guide, Annabella, who will speak through me," I said. "Do not be alarmed if my voice changes and I sound child-like. She was very young when she passed away in this house, a victim of the cholera epidemic."

"Is there anything sadder than a girl whose race is over before she gets out of the gate?" said Case.

"*Très triste*," said the Captain. "One could weep."

"Annabella is quite merry," said Willie. "Dearly loves a riddle, the little imp."

"Can't get the grasp of the trifecta," said Bertie. "Never had a chance to learn basic arithmetic."

"Please take the hand of those next to you and close your eyes," I said, joining hands with Willie and the Captain. "We shall sing a nursery rhyme to call to Annabella."

As the little song lilted up (Bertie has a lovely tenor) I felt an immediate shift in the cosmic sphere. This was an extraordinarily interconnected group, the most powerful I've encountered. I nearly swooned as I felt the psychic energy surge from person to person. Halfway through the first verse we tore a hole in the veil and the table bounced up and down.

"Do not break the circle," I said as all eyes flew open. Their faces glowed in the flickering candlelight, floating above the now still table as if disembodied.

"Astonishing," said Willie. "It usually takes several choruses and much coaxing for Annabella to make herself known."

"Perhaps there will finally be news of a winner," said Bertie. "You have brought me luck, young Case."

"Annabella has never moved the table," said Willie. "The poor child does not have the strength."

"I didn't do it," Annabella's voice spoke through me. "There is someone else."

"Who is it?" said Willie.

"Whom do you seek?" said Annabella.

"It's Hattie," said Case. "She would do anything to get to the front of a line. That's how she met the secret lover, with a crazy Red Cross routine to meet the men, or at least the handsome ones, coming back from flight training at Camp Borden. Decked herself out in a nurse's uniform to meet the planes as they landed and pranced onto the runway. It was glorious."

"I don't like her," said Annabella.

"Don't worry Annabella, Hattie adores children," said Case. "She wanted a whole stable, was always picking out baby names."

We jumped as a loud rap sounded on the table.

"Annabella never raps," said Willie.

"It's not me," said Annabella. "It's someone naughty. Go away naughty spirit."

The table was rapped again, hard, and Willie and the Captain gripped my hands more tightly.

"One rap for no, two for yes," said Bertie. "Do you have a message for me about the Queen's Plate? Or even the Breeder's Stakes?"

Rap.

"Is it for me?" said Willie. "Mother?"

Rap.

"I'm frightened," said Annabella.

"Don't be afraid, little Bella," said Willie, his hand shaking in mine.

"I see her!" said Case.

"Annabella?" said Willie.

"Hattie!" said Case, staring into the darkness. "She's right there. Can't you see her? She's like a dancing mouse, whirling and twirling. Don't you see her, *mon capitaine*? She is right behind you."

The Captain did not turn his head. "There is nothing to see," he said.

"I miss you, Hattie. Everyone does," said Case. "Your parents. Your chums. The crowd at the Dollar Bill Club. Even the shops on Brock Street miss you. They're still buzzing about how you waltzed into Bibby's to buy the dress Mama Dressler wore in her last moving picture. You said little things help a look along, but not that get-up – baggy, bows, ribbons and the most horrifying pink. Pink!"

93

The table moved again, bumping up and down.

"The spirits are angry," said Annabella.

"I'm angry, Hattie," said Case. "I'm angry they say you took your own life. I thought you were finally getting down to living it when you swore off martinis and driving too fast and scotched our scheme to dress like bellhops to get Valentino's autograph."

"Perhaps," said Bertie, "she was putting her affairs in order."

"Hattie, I must know," said Case "Why buy matronly dresses and give up booze and fast cars? Why ask the secret lover to leave his wife?"

The table bounced up and down, more violently now, but still we held fast to the circle.

"Was there a baby?" said Case.

Rap-rap.

"Is that why your family thinks you topped yourself?" said Case.

Rap-rap.

"They think you died of shame? Shame! I'm happy to say you do not know the meaning of the word."

Rap-rap.

"Incredible!" said Willie.

"Did you shuffle yourself off this mortal hootenanny?" said Case.

Rap.

"Was it an accident?" said Case.

Rap.

"Murder?"

Rap-rap. Rap-Rap. RAP-RAP! RAP-RAP!

"Who did it?" said Willie. "Who murdered you, Hattie?"

"She is reaching out!" said Case. "She is —"

The girl lurched forward in her seat, writhing and thrashing, but still holding tight to Willie and Bertie.

"She is possessed," said Willie, with a look of admiration I did not like.

"Bloody hell," said Bertie.

"I don't want to play anymore," said Annabella, starting to cry.

Case sat bolt upright, still clutching hands with the men next to her, and began to gag. I fretted that, for the first time at one of my channelings, ectoplasm would gush forth and certainly stain the linen tablecloth. But, instead of thick, green mucus, a small golden charm emerged between the girl's pursed lips. Tiny flashes of light seemed to spark from it as it flew from her mouth and landed, wheels down, on the tablecloth in front of the Captain.

The room went silent.

Then the table shot up and flipped over, forcing our hands apart. The candle toppled sideways onto the floor and ignited the beeswax-soaked tablecloth. Flames from the blazing linen spread quickly to my best rug, the red wool the lumber baron brought back from Persia. I ran for the light switch (the lumber baron liked all the modern conveniences) and flicked it on to see Willie in his shirtsleeves and waistcoat, beating at the fire with his jacket. Case knelt on the floor, reaching for the airplane charm glinting in the reflected light of the flames. Bertie ran out, the waiting room curtains flapping in his wake. The Captain stood holding a Webley six-shot revolver, the same make of pistol my first husband took into the clouds over France.

Then the psychic energy in the room exploded like an over-stoked steam locomotive going down a mighty grade and jolted me into a telepathic vision. As the smoke swirled, flames crackled, and Willie called for water, my salon faded away and I saw myself standing in a cleared field on a moon-lit night. Captain St. Pierre wore a thick wool coat and heavy scarf as he stood beside a Sopwith Camel and loaded bullets into his pistol. His goggles were drawn back over the leather cap on his forehead, his large dark eyes shone in the moonlight, and I wondered how I ever thought them sad. He loaded the final bullet into the chamber and said, "Contact."

Then I heard my first husband speak through me. "It's no good, man," his voice said. "This dogfight is over. You're grounded."

My vision cleared and I was back in my salon, those big eyes staring at me over the pistol barrel. The Captain kept the gun pointed at me as he slowly turned his head to Willie, still beating at the fire with his ruined jacket, and then to the girl cupping the airplane charm in her hands. He thumbed back the hammer of the gun.

The waiting room curtains fluttered again and Bertie raced back into the room carrying the large Wedgewood pitcher the lumber baron bought as part of our wedding china. The Captain turned at Bertie's entrance so that the pistol pointed at my upright Richardson piano (a gift from the widow of the company's owner). Bertie tossed water from the pitcher at the flaming rug, thoroughly soaking Willie, and took a quick step back to smash the pitcher on the side of the Captain's head. The pitcher shattered, the Captain dropped the pistol, a bullet tore into my piano, and musical notes echoed like the waning peals of church bells after a funeral. As the Captain sprang for his weapon, Bertie snatched up one of the rosewood chairs and knocked him out cold.

"He was certainly a dark horse," said Bertie, picking up the pistol and pointing it at the prone figure on the floor.

"Astonishing!" said Willie, wiping his forehead with his handkerchief. "I need the use of your telephone, madame, to contact the authorities."

"Thank you, Willie," said Case. "I was hoping you'd say that."

"Anything for you, young lady," said Willie. "You are a most powerful medium."

"Powerful and young, yes. A lady, maybe," said Case. "But a medium? No."

"I don't understand," said Willie.

"As my cousin Artie says, once you have eliminated the impossible, whatever remains must be the real poop," she said. "There were no spirits. I faked it."

"The fix was in," said Bertie. "It always is."

"I am no fake," I said. "My psychic abilities are acknowledged in the highest circles. My mother was spiritual advisor to the Duchess of Argyle."

"How lovely if it were all true," said Case. "I like to think boys I knew before the War are whooping it up in the clouds and waiting for my long-distance call. But there's a problem with the operator given the cholera epidemic was in 1837 and this house wasn't built until 50 years later."

"A minor blunder on Annabella's part," I said. "Children get muddled about time on the other side."

"One could say that," said Case.

"This is most confounding," said Willie. "If not for the spirits, how could you know these things?"

"Hattie told me," said Case, "while she was alive. She rattled on about the handsome Captain leaving his wife, the golden charm, long journeys to romantic places, and children with large brown eyes. She could not shut up about the secret lover."

"But how did you know he would be here?" said Willie.

"I made sure he'd lose a bet," said Case. "The folks at Dollar Bills adored Hattie even more than gambling."

"A longshot comes in," said Bertie. The pistol never wavered as he straightened his tie then slid his damaged hand into his pocket.

"It was elementary," said Case. "I followed Cousin Artie's method, which is founded on the observation of trifles. And I do love trifles."

# Crown Witness

**The Pitchfork Murder Trial** was to be my greatest triumph. As chief witness for the Crown, the courtroom drama would revolve around me. A hush would fall over the courtroom as I entered, ladies' ivory fans stalling mid-swish, gentlemen rising to doff top hats. All eyes would be on me as I testified in a ladylike voice, demure yet strong enough to carry to the newspaper man scribbling down every word. I would be the courtroom sensation of 1838.

It was high time. In the three years since my brother took out the newspaper advertisement announcing "John A. Macdonald, Attorney and Etc," I've toiled in obscurity for the courts of Upper Canada. There can be little doubt I am the greatest "Etc" the law here has ever seen, an expert in the legal skullduggery best suited to a homely spinster sister. I trade gossip, snoop in cupboards, poke about people's affairs, conjugal and otherwise, all the back-door shenanigans that help a rising young lawyer win cases. But this time the newspaper story would be all about me, not my clever older brother and his courtroom speeches.

I should have known better. I've spent enough time in Johnny's law office to know "witness" is another word for "bystander." And then there was the family question, as Johnny pointed out while I prepared breakfast the morning of the trial.

"It's unnatural, Louisa," he said, as I stirred the lumpy oatmeal burping in the pot. "You and I can't be on opposite sides of the fence."

What? You think it a conflict for me to testify for the Crown while Johnny acts for the defence? Well, that's Kingston for you. Throw a stick down Brock Street and you'll hit someone related by blood or marriage. And I swear, I had told my brother nothing of what I witnessed that day.

"Don't fret," I sniffed, turning from the pot, careful not to slop on the frock I had carefully pressed that morning for my public appearance. "My little story won't sully your budding reputation as a great orator."

"You and I are always on the same side," coaxed Johnny, shaking his big head. "Even when we were children. Remember how we played at marching to Waterloo?"

"I marched. You were Wellington on his horse," I said, pouring the weak tea. "And family ties complicate things. You'd have an easier time in court if your client's family was less devoted."

"Perhaps the Boisverts were a wee bit carried away by brotherly love," Johnny admitted over the chipped mug I handed him.

When the blacksmith Antoine Boisvert was charged with the pitchfork murder of his wife, three of his brothers eagerly vouched for his whereabouts during the crime. Unfortunately, they provided three conflicting alibis, leaving Johnny with an interesting dilemma.

"Have you decided which tale you prefer?" I asked, sipping from the finer china cup I reserved for myself.

"Perhaps Antoine rode out to fix a broken wagon wheel for his brother Michel's stagecoach," Johnny said. "That puts him well out of town during the crime."

"So does building a henhouse at his brother Hubert's farm," I said.

"On the other hand," Johnny reflected, "the harbormaster saw two men rowing out to the American steamship which Antoine and brother Jacques supplied with new rope."

"From a distance," I noted, "the Boisverts are as alike as peas in a pod."

Johnny raised a shaggy eyebrow and muttered about family resemblances and loyalties and things running skin deep.

"Save it for the judge," I said, turning to find the oat-meal scorched and stuck hard to the bottom of the pot. There was no breakfast in the Macdonald house that morning and we were both in a foul humour when we arrived at the courthouse.

"Good luck, Lou," Johnny said, turning to the Clarence Street side door reserved for officers of the court. "Remember, the judge prefers a ladylike voice."

"My speaking voice is perfectly modulated!" I shouted at my brother's retreating back.

I felt surprisingly small as I turned alone to the court-house's double front doors. It was a hot, close July morning and life's rich pageant spilled about me, unseemly vivacious on what I felt should be a solemn day. A steam whistle sounded cheerfully in the harbour, chickens squawked in the market square, and from every direction came the hammering and sawing that is the melody of our rising town.

Hopping up the front step, I smelled the linseed oil of fresh paint and looked up to see a painter buoyed by a rope as he gave the courthouse cupola a much-needed freshening up. About time, too. Once the pride of Kingston, our courthouse is tatty after forty years of hard labour. There is talk of replacing it with a magnificent limestone building on a site with its own park, well away from the muck of downtown. What a grand idea, I thought as I ambled through the front entrance, to move the scales of justice far from the stink I could smell wafting in from the British American Hotel's stables across the road.

As I put my foot on the bottom stair leading up to the second-floor courtroom, I heard my name being called by the bailiff. Johnny had timed our arrival too closely, no doubt as retribution for the oatmeal, and I took the stairs at an ungainly trot, bursting gracelessly into the court-room. My fresh frock was stained with sweat and my face red and shiny, much to the amusement of the spectators shifting noisily on the hard pine benches.

The stench of the stable seemed to grow stronger as I neared the witness stand at the front of the room. My last thoughts of courtroom glamour fell away as I clapped eyes on the stinkiest bailiff in the Canadas. While I toiled in un-paid anonymity as the law's greatest Etc, Winkie Dudgeon had saved the traveling judge from an unscrupulous horse trader and been rewarded with a job in the Kingston court.

Winkie yawned, rubbed his good eye, and thrust out a shop-worn Bible tatty from four decades of contact with the palms of villains. The judge idly scratched his chest under his heavy black robe, the Crown squinted over a note, and Johnny turned in his wrinkled black gown (there was no time to press it after I finished my frock) and bent his head to whisper to his client.

Antoine Boisvert, a good foot shorter than my lanky brother, looked an unlikely murderer — indeed, he looked an unlikely blacksmith. Like all the Boisverts he was a small, wiry fellow, not the hulking behemoth one reads about in epic poems. He had a pleasant freckled face, tidy and straight dark hair, and was dressed in spotless Sunday blacks with a clean white shirt. Long sleeves peeped out

103

under his coat, the cuffs almost covering the manacles clamped there. I wondered if Antoine had forged the iron bonds on his own wrists.

The Boisverts had built much of Kingston since arriving at the naval yards during the War with the Americans. They were a hardworking clan, good with tools and live-stock, conversing in nimble French with each other and parsimonious English when about their business. They built buildings or chopped wood or hauled water or paint-ed window sashes, all their deals sealed with a handshake. (If all of Kingston were so honest, there would be much less work for John A. Macdonald and Etc). But if one Bois-vert dropped from the gallows, he would take the family's reputation down with him.

As I surveyed the unwashed rabble that made up the courtroom spectators, I saw the brothers Boisvert were absent. *C'est la vie*, I thought, the only French phrase I know. What good was having the fastest team of horses to reach Bytown, or the plumpest chickens in the market, or the thickest rope in the harbour, when the whole town shuns your family for the murderer in its midst? Best to shun him first.

Murderer or not, I felt a pang for Antoine as he leaned forward to catch the English words. The aromatic Winkie came to the end of his recitation of the oath and grunted, "So help you, by God?"

"I do," I said roundly. A wag in the crowd loudly de-clared this my only chance to utter that phrase, a detail underscored by the Crown insisting I identify myself to the court as "spinster," and the crowd burst into laughter.

I well know this town thinks me blunt and homely while Johnny's face – twin to mine! – is full of wit and character. My brother will go far, the town says, but I am a thin-lipped mouth he must feed. But as Johnny scowled at the laughter and curled his long fingers into fists, I wished I had taken more care with his oatmeal.

"Miss Macdonald," the Crown said. "Please tell the court about the morning of the second of June."

"I went to the tea merchant," I spoke quietly. "We still had green tea in the house but my father drank the last of the Souchong and we like –."

The Crown interrupted. "Perhaps if you could come to the matter before the court?"

"Of course," I said, a gentle cough conveying my awareness that such testimony could strain a woman of delicate sensibilities.

"Perhaps such testimony is too much for this witness's delicate sensibilities," said my brother, leaping to his hind legs.

"It is my duty to continue," I sighed quickly.

"Please do," said the Judge, "and stop mumbling. I can scarcely hear you over that din in the market."

Realizing that Johnny had laid a trap for me with his warning about soft speech, I abandoned any regrets about his oatmeal and raised my voice. And indeed, the sound of the market chickens had grown louder, as if they were flying up to roost on the courthouse roof.

"I was headed home past the blacksmith shop when I stopped to speak with Mrs. Cobb, who was recommending a new compound to cleanse the skin –."

"Did Mrs. Cobb see anything at the smithy?" asked the Crown.

"I doubt it," I said. "The stage came roaring down the street raising a dreadful cloud of dust. She was concerned about grit blemishing her complexion and hurried in-doors."

As if to underscore my story, outside a team of horses stamped and jingled in their traces as the stage pulled up to the hotel. If Antoine heard his brother's team, he made no sign, twiddling his thumbs as if his manacled hands did not know how to be idle.

The noise, however, was too distracting for the judge, who ordered Winkie to close the windows, shutting off all chance of a fresh breeze. I continued my testimony with my nose pointed away from the bailiff.

"As I drew near the forge I heard her," I said, giving a shiver as I got to the nub of the tale.

"Your honour, the witness appears to have a chill." My brother hopped up again. "Given the sweltering heat, I am concerned for her health."

"I am quite well," I said soundly.

"Then get on with it," said the Judge.

"I heard shouting from the smithy. Now, I am no nosey old puss (another chortle from the crowd) but the loud voices startled me."

"What did you hear?" asked the Crown.

"Mrs. Boisvert was shouting at someone."

"What was she arguing about?"

"The witness said she overheard shouting, not arguing," interjected Johnny.

"Shouting, then," said the Crown, conceding the point with a small wave.

"She said, "Get that mangy horseflesh out of here. I've no time for your filthy schemes." I paused as the newspaper man began to scribble. About time, too.

"What else did the deceased say?" asked the Crown.

"The woman was hardly deceased at the time," observed Johnny, who is devilishly quick. I moved on before he could slow my tale further.

"She said, 'Stop giving me the evil eye. I'd rather die than try such a dirty trick. The whole town will know about you before this is done.' "

"Your witness, Mr. Macdonald," said the Crown, plunking into his seat. He, too, was no stranger to dramatic effect.

"Those were her exact words?" Johnny asked slowly as he rose to his feet. " 'I would rather die.' "

"Her exact words," I repeated.

"How do you know?" Johnny asked.

"Because I heard them," I said cheekily, but I saw the look on Johnny's face. He had the same look when we played Duke of Wellington and he thought up a new plan for taking Waterloo.

"Do you speak French?" he said.

"You know I don't."

"So Mrs. Boisvert was speaking English?"

"She must have been," said the judge, "if your sister knows no French."

"Miss Macdonald, if you are able, could you tell the court," said Johnny, drawing it out, "why a French woman would speak English to her French husband?"

He had me. I am certain Johnny would have resolved the whole thing there, but then one of the courtroom windows was smashed and the first of the chickens shot through.

It caused a great commotion as birds dropped through the window one by one, frantically puffing out their feathers and squawking and flapping about the courtroom. There was much laughter, too, and the wag made a joke about scrawny old birds too tough for the pot. Old bird was harsh – I am only 20 years old – and I was about to make a sharp retort when I remembered chickens cannot fly.

Someone was reaching down from the cupola and tossing the birds into the courtroom. It was a canny distraction, for not only did the frantic birds bring my vital testimony to a halt, more than one courtroom spectator availed himself of a free fowl and headed towards the staircase. The result was like a cork thrust into a bottle. The stairway was jammed as those trying to get down met people from the lower floor coming up to see what was causing the hullabaloo. That was when I realized where things were heading.

"Johnny!" I shouted. "Make them see before it's too late!"

"Order, order!" shouted the Judge, pounding his gavel. The bailiff grabbed me roughly by the arm and dragged me from the witness stand. I tossed aside my last shred of dignity to twist and scratch until he dropped me. I landed on the floor with my crumpled skirt over my head, rolling about in the waste that inevitably flows from agitated chickens.

"Stop him, Johnny!" I shouted.

That was when Jacques Boisvert swung through the second-storey window brandishing an axe. He was a small man, too, and had no trouble sliding through the broken pane. His wiry arms bulged menacingly as he strolled calmly through the chaos of the courtroom and up to the defendant's table.

"Stop!" cried Johnny. "There's no need!"

Antoine did not hesitate at the sight of his brother's approach. Leaning forward in his chair, he spread his arms wide on the table and nodded. Jacques nodded back, raised the axe over his head, and with one quick chop the chains fell in pieces.

"*Arretez-vous*!" tried Johnny, who had picked up a few words at the Chateau Quebec, the city's largest French Canadian tavern. (My brother plays no favourites when it comes to local publicans.) Tossing Winkie aside, Johnny pumped his long legs to beat the axe-wielding Boisverts to the window, where a thick rope dangled outside from the cupola. I had no doubt that on the ground below brother

Michel waited with his stagecoach and the fastest team of horses in Kingston.

"Stop!" shouted Johnny, raising his hands. "If you run I cannot help you!"

If I were the Boisverts I would have made good my escape. I saw the need to run, understandable in any language, writ large across their faces. Jacques was tightening his grip on the axe, his arms tensing for a mighty swing, when I dashed through the chicken feathers and broken glass to throw myself in front of my brother.

"Who was it, Monsieur Boisvert?" I cried. "Who came to you speaking English? Who is dirty and has an evil eye? Who does shady deals with horses?"

At my words Johnny stopped his attempt to toss me out of harm's way, and he and Antoine turned their heads together to look back into the courtroom.

"That man," said Antoine. Raising his wrist, the severed manacle dangling like a bracelet, he pointed to Winkie, who stood near the stairway with a chicken under each arm. "He asked me to shoe a lame horse with a trick. He says we can sell many sick horses." And then came a flood of French better suited for the Chateau Quebec.

It would have saved a lot of bother, and some chickens, if I had talked to my brother before the trial. The Boisverts would not have had to commit their first crime by attempting a jailbreak. Luckily, the judge is inclined to let them off lightly, given that he hired Winkie as bailiff. Things can't die down fast enough for His Honour, now that the newspaper has printed three stories. Not a single one mentioned my name.

# Sister Companion

The snow had turned to icy beads that should
have stung my face but I could scarce distinguish them
from the tears flowing down my cheeks. The white garni-
ture designed to modestly cover my head hung in a sodden mass about my neck, my hair was plastered to my
head, and my thick woollen cloak hung heavily about me
like a great black blanket as I lashed the lines against the
horses to urge them to greater speed.

Surely the others were as cold and frightened as I, but
they gave no sign. Behind me Mother Anthony worked
calmly to cushion Mr. Toomey against the bumping of the
sleigh. Mr. Toomey mumbled curses – words he might

have roared in front of anyone but two nuns – and tried to make little of the shotgun wound to his shoulder.

"A scratch," he said. "Don't need a woman driving."

"Nonsense," said Mother Anthony in the gentle but firm tone she usually reserved for novices and the bishop. "Sister Mary is perfectly capable of driving the horses."

"I drove a team of four after the boys left the farm," I said heartily over my shoulder, hoping they would not notice my tears amid the snowdrops.

Mr. Toomey struggled to push off the bulky travelling blanket but Mother Anthony, a substantial woman who outweighed him by a good fifty pounds, forcefully tucked him back in. "You must keep still to stem the bleeding," she chided him. "It will be some time before we reach a doctor."

"No doctor," Mr. Toomey said. "Been in worse spots. Lived to tell it."

Certainly his appearance gave that credence, for it looked as if he had lived every one of his forty-odd years. A nasty scar dashed up the left side of his misshapen face, ending in a patch that would have been black had it not been dirty grey. He had lost the eye when a horse kicked him during a shoeing – and that was almost all we knew of him, for Mr. Toomey was a reserved man who never spoke of himself or his people. We were sure, however, that the Lord sent him to us for a reason.

We had waited till after the fall harvest to begin begging alms for the residence for the aged that our city needed so desperately. Despite the size of our diocese, we

114

had soon exhausted the financial prospects of our parishes and were forced to travel far afield to gather funds. Several men had then petitioned to drive Mother Anthony and I, her sister companion, on the collecting tour that would take us hundreds of cold miles from home.

While rough in appearance, Mr. Toomey stood out from the others in the test Mother Anthony had devised. She asked all to run the horses up the lane behind our Motherhouse, a finely appointed building somewhat off the Montreal Road on the outskirts of the city. They were to stop on the bluff from which we could see the big lake. The others had come as close to the bluff's edge as possible to show their skill in managing the horses. Mr. Toomey, however, had pulled up several yards away, mindful of the safety of his would-be passengers. I was not surprised he was chosen to accompany us on our journey.

As our journey progressed it became clear Mother Anthony was a good judge of character. We had ranged far, south into Buffalo and through the United States, then back into Canada and north to Ottawa, the new capital. Throughout our travels Mr. Toomey had shown great fortitude, particularly when our sleigh crashed through the ice as we passed through the Thousand Islands. I had thought all was lost but, in the blink of an eye, Mr. Toomey had cut the horses from the traces, saving both passengers and beasts. He had spent the next day begging, in his taciturn way, and the result was a sleigh better than the one we had lost.

Indeed, he was a man of many resources and had kept our horses steady while Mother Anthony had kept faith in our mission. Bit by bit Providence had prevailed through their labour and we had sent some hard-won money home.

The final few days of our expedition, however, had seen little success. As we returned through the north we found no friends in such Methodist hamlets as Fisherville, Newtonbrook and Willowdale and even the inhabitants of O'Sullivan's Corners proved to be staunch supporters of the Orange Lodge. We had just about given up hope when we met with a final, unexpected success.

It being Sunday we had stopped for Mass at St. Columbine's, just a few hours from our Motherhouse, and found the congregation had not been idle in our absence. In full support of our cause, they had held a raffle raising the princely sum of $800. With much thanks Mother Anthony had gathered it to her purse, giving no thought to carrying such a sum with our final destination so close at hand.

Disaster had struck as we were passing a sharp bend at the Three Corners. A cut-throat, a flour sack over his head and an ugly weapon in his hand, stood up in the snow.

"Throw down your purse," he ordered, casually aiming a shot gun like my brother Earl had used on the farm. Later I found all I could remember of his appearance was that he handled the weapon with a maddening composure.

"Steal from the church and from women of God!" Mother Anthony said sternly, no fear in her voice. "You should be ashamed."

"Shame don't enter into it," replied the cut-throat, making a motion with the gun barrel. "Throw it down."

"Can't reason with such a one," Mr. Toomey said in the sharp, raspy voice I had heard frighten a hostler who tried to cheat us in Ottawa. "Give up."

"That's right, friend," said the bandit. "Let the good sister throw down her money."

"You shall not have it!" Mother Anthony said. "There are eleven infirm men in our wards who need this money to die in some peace and comfort."

"Those men die will poor with or without that money," said the cut-throat. "Throw it down."

"You're a terrible sinner," Mother Anthony said, and it seemed she was pulling her purse from her pocket. But, with a quickness astonishing in a woman of her proportions, she grabbed the whip that sat upright next to Mr. Toomey and snapped it at the bandit.

As the whip cracked Mr. Toomey threw himself in front of us. The blast from the gun caught him in the shoulder, propelling him back into our laps, and the spooked horses took off at a gallop. Mr. Toomey held to the lines with one hand to keep them from running free under the sleigh as Mother Anthony swiftly attempted to wrest them from him, shouting for me to scramble into the driver's seat.

It seemed an impossible task and I directed my prayers to St. Jude as I tumbled into place, my skirts a muddle on the snow-slick bench. I was barely upright before Mother Anthony gave the lines over to me and I began to pull back.

"No! Faster!" shouted Mother Anthony. "We must flee!"

I had not thought of the bandit's pursuit, only of stopping the horses before we overturned. Now I lashed at the team, calling to them as I had heard my brothers shout when they raced father's best pair at the fall exhibition. But our horses were a working pair, not bred for speed, and as I looked behind me I saw a dark figure gaining despite the slippery purchase.

I lashed again at the beasts, already trying their best to slither up a hill, when there was a yell from Mr. Toomey. I turned to glimpse him flinging Mother Anthony's purse onto the road.

"Stop! Whoa!" shouted Mother Anthony.

"G'up!" yelled Mr. Toomey and the horses began to pull even harder at the sound of his voice. When I was able to turn back a second time the bandit had disappeared.

"You should not have done that," Mother Anthony said angrily. "You had no authority."

"Must see you home safe."

"The Lord would have protected us!"

"He did," said Mr. Toomey, and that set Mother Anthony back. After months of using her wit and skill to do the Lord's work, she saw the sense of it.

"We may get it back," she said finally. "The police will soon catch the bandit."

"No police," said Mr. Toomey.

"Surely you do not expect such a crime to go unreported!"

"I tossed the money. They'll wonder 'bout me," said Mr. Toomey, who knew the ways of men well enough. "Won't do."

The next few miles were anxious and it was with great relief that I pulled up the nearly spent team in front of the Motherhouse. I was young in those days, little more than a girl, and it was nothing for me to make an undignified leap from the seat. I skittered forward in the icy road, my skirt gathered in my hand, to steady the team as Mother Anthony helped Mr. Toomey from the sleigh. He was a small man, just two inches taller than my own five feet two, and slim and wiry. Now he looked runty beside the queenly proportions of our black-cloaked superior.

Our arrival home would have caused a stir in any event and it was no surprise to see our sisters come running to greet us. Their looks of joy turned quickly to concern, but it was a time for action, not explanation.

"We met with trouble on the road," said Mother Anthony. "Sister Mary must be warmed up and dressed in a fresh habit, and do not plague her with questions."

I left the care of the horses, who had done a mighty job, to two sisters who had also been raised on the farm. Then I hurried gratefully towards warm water and a clean habit. The sisters were bursting to query me but obeyed Mother Anthony's instructions and, indeed, I was too exhausted to speak. As I waited for the water to heat, I knelt to thank God for guiding my hands on the lines and asked him to keep Mr. Toomey safe from his wounds.

I had only the one habit and so was fastening my rosary to borrowed garments when I was summoned to our front parlour. It was the first time I was to sit in the good parlour, although as a novice I had spent some hours cleaning the marble fireplace. There I found Mr. Toomey and Mother Anthony with Constable O'Reilly.

I was not surprised to see the young policeman. Our city was a much smaller place in those days and someone must have seen our wild race through the snow and felt it merited the attention of the officials.

"The damn–, oddest thing," Mr. Toomey was saying. "Had Bess's hoof in hand hundred times a'fore."

Mr. Toomey looked even smaller without his snow-covered muffler, great coat, and cap. His blue jeans, a bit too long, were turned up to reveal the cuffs of a rather good pair of wool trousers which he wore to Mass on Sundays. His shoulder was bound and, though he must have been in great pain, his funny rasp of a voice never quaked.

"Come in, Sister Mary," said Mother Anthony, looking up from the silver tea service which the bishop's sister had bequeathed to us. "Mr. Toomey has been telling the constable how he injured himself."

Puzzling over her uncharitable description of what could be described as rash behaviour on her part but certainly not Mr. Toomey's, I sat on the embroidered chair they had left for me near the fire.

"Good afternoon, Sister Mary," said Constable O'Reilly, balancing one of our best china cups on his knee. "I understand you have had quite a fright."

"Fright does not describe it," I said.

"Indeed," Mother Anthony took over. "To think we travelled so far without incident and then had such an accident close to home. And that so much could come of a horse throwing a shoe! Thanks be to God we arrived here safely."

I was astonished at her words but kept chastity of my eyes, staring down into the teacup she had presented me.

"You may have been very fortunate, sisters," Constable O'Reilly said. "There have been several robberies on the Montreal Road these past few months."

"Alas, we had nothing to steal," said Mother Anthony. "Our travels have not given us the bounty we were seeking. We were returning empty-handed."

Mindful of my vow of obedience I mutely sipped my tea, hoping Mother Anthony's meaning would be made clear. Did she fear others would think Mr. Toomey had tossed our money at the bandit as a conspirator? Perhaps the constable sensed my discomfort, for he certainly did not suspect Mother Anthony of deception. He was from a fine church-going family and could not conceive of a sister telling an untruth. And truly, when he inquired how I felt, I replied honestly.

"I thank the Lord I did not overturn the sleigh," I said.

"It seems you have some talent as a driver," Constable O'Reilly said. "Perhaps you will be able to give Mr. Toomey some lessons."

Mother Anthony gave a small laugh at his joke and more polite talk was exchanged, but the constable was a busy man and he soon finished up his tea and left. He was barely out the door when Mr. Toomey slumped forward, allowing the strain to appear on his pale face. He seemed to weigh almost nothing as Mother Anthony and I carried him to her office, where a bowl of hot water and some clean cloths sat waiting on her desk.

"I need assistance cleaning Mr. Toomey's wound," said Mother Anthony. "I trust that what you see and hear shall remain between the three of us and God."

"Of course, Mother Anthony," I said.

"Sister Mary." Mr. Toomey's squeak was now thin with pain. "Hear my story."

"There's no need," I said. "I am sure that you have always been a good Christian gentleman."

"No," he said with a small laugh, the only one I ever heard him give. "Born on farm, like you. Hard work, but always food and such. Was twelve when pa lost the farm."

It was a long speech for him, but he continued. "Too proud for poorhouse. Went to town. No work. Much handsomer creature then. Might've took bad ways."

I was unsure of his meaning. I knew of grinding poverty and the poor nameless babes who showed up at our door. But I had not yet seen all the evil that Satan can work and that a boy could be used so foully did not occur to me.

"Liked horses," he went on. "Work 'em ways others can't. Worked lots of places. Like it here. Don't want to move on."

The bell that guided the Motherhouse through the day rang for the evening prayer and Mr. Toomey took it as a signal to end his story. I was more confused than ever as I stood by Mother Anthony and prepared to help clean shot and bits of wool shirt from the nasty wound.

People think we sisters lead sheltered lives but our cloister is the world and as we nurse its sick and dying we see much of the world's mortification. Still, I was unprepared as Mother Anthony pulled Mr. Toomey's shirt from his back. My hands started involuntarily, nearly knocking the water basin to the floor.

"Steady, Sister Mary," Mother Anthony said.

Those were the last words we ever spoke on the subject.

I kept Mr. Toomey's secret until his death causes me to share it with you, your Grace. You have often encountered Mr. Toomey, as I find I still refer to him, as he drove us about, even in these late days when the Lord has seen fit for me to assume the role of Mother Superior. I believe he has even driven you when your man was indisposed.

Now we find he has left his savings to our home for the aged, after already paying us many times over for the $800 Mother Anthony sacrificed for him. But truly, it was no sacrifice. Of course, he would have been cleared by an inquiry but appearances would have dictated he no longer serve the Lord with us at the Motherhouse, and he has been a good and faithful servant.

And what safer place was there for such a person than a convent? There was no sin in the fact that Mr. Toomey was a woman. I'm sure there is no reason he – I must learn to say she – cannot lie in consecrated ground.

# *Marley Was Dead*

## Marley was dead.

"Dead as a doornail," said my brother Clayton. "No doubt about it."

Of course Marley was dead. I knew it. Clayton knew it. A third of the volunteer fire department knew it. Soon, the entire township would know it. We had worked on Marley for a good twenty minutes – mouth-to-mouth, oxygen, chest compressions, even the new defibrillator we got with a grant from the province.

"Old Marley is as dead as doornail," said our friend Pete, as he peeled the defibrillator tabs from Marley's chest.

Clayton looked down at his hockey stick lying next to Marley's body on the floor of the township firehall. "I can't believe it," he said, "Mayor Jacob P. Marley, the day of the Santa Claus parade, killed in our firehall. Killed with my hockey stick! It's just wrong. That was my best road hockey stick, an Easton Magnum, the wooden Sakic model, made right here in Canada, it's …"

Clayton kept talking and I kept looking at the body. It was Jacob Marley to the life – well, to the death. His long chain of office spread out behind him like a tail. We'd tossed it aside while we tried resuscitation. He still wore his usual desert boots, his usual leather jacket, his usual ponytail, the one the newspaper called "brave" in that story before the last election. There was a blue-red gash over his left eye, the only mark on him. The killer blow to the head had not broken Marley's glasses. The wire rims were still pushed back on his balding forehead in a way we knew well, for Marley was a fine-print man, with a keen eye for numbers and details. He'd been proud of the grant application he had written for the defibrillator.

"… I thought for sure Marley's defibrillator would do the trick," Clayton finished. "If he wasn't dead, this would kill him. I hope we used it right."

"We used it right," I said.

"Did we use it right?" said Pete Repeat, his nickname since Grade Three.

"We used it right," I said. "You can't shock a bludgeoned man back to life. There was no way it would work."

"You never know," said Clayton.

"Yes, you do," I said.

"Well, I was hoping," said Clayton.

"I was hoping, too," said Pete.

"Well," I said. "Me, too."

We were quiet for a minute. Even Clayton. When we arrived at the firehall to set up our after-parade open house and found Marley lying on the floor, our training kicked in, not surprisingly. Mostly all we did was train. But we didn't like what our training told us to do next.

"We have to call the police," I said.

"Not those bastards," said Clayton.

"Bastards," said Pete.

The rivalry between the volunteer fire department and the township police had been almost friendly. Then Marley figured out disbanding the force for a contract with the Ontario Provincial Police meant the township could afford a second fire truck and increase our property save rate by twenty-two per cent. It looked like a done deal until the police launched their public relations campaign.

First, they swept the Township Hockey Series four games straight with The Ringer, a quiet rookie constable who'd flunked provincial police college but whose wicked slapshot had taken him to Junior A in the Ontario Hockey League. He scored a hat trick in the first period of Game One against Marley, who was in goal for Fire. Marley, ever the sportsman, vowed to practice more. But the bastards were just getting started. With the township budget vote scheduled for year end, they spent weeks appealing to voters by helping every charity within twenty miles, hosting fish fries, ham suppers, bake sales, and 50-50 draws.

We thought Fire had a lock on the Santa Claus parade. Our red engine, Pumper One, trumped the snowmobile on a trailer the police towed down the main street. Wearing hockey sweaters from the Township Series was a parade tradition, too, and our red and white was a lot more Christmas-y than the police shamrock green. And the parade always ended at the firehall, with an open house, hot chocolate, and a game of road hockey, Fire versus the Prince Charles High School Royales.

But this year, marching behind the police snowmobile, was a Toronto police pipe and drum band that won third place three years in a row in the big city Santa Claus parade. After the parade they planned to play Christmas carols in the firehall parking lot while the local cops sold souvenir pucks to raise money for the Royales to visit the national Hockey Hall of Fame. They really were bastards.

"Do we need them?" said Clayton.

"We don't need them," said Pete.

"Marley was murdered," I said.

"Marley would say there's nothing in the fine print that says we have to call right away," said Clayton. "At least give us a head start."

"We got fifteen minutes," I said, dialing 9-1-1. "That's how long it takes them to unhitch the snowmobile trailer and back out of the parade."

"Twenty," said Clayton. "They always have trouble with that hitch."

The call was quick. I said Jacob Marley was dead in the firehall. They said not to touch anything. I hung up.

"Don't touch anything," I said.

Then the woman I loved threw open the firehall door and dragged in a six-foot bundle bound in blue tarp and duct tape. She wrestled the bundle inside, turned to see Marley, and dropped the bundle on the floor, branches of a Christmas tree ripping through the canvas.

"Marley is dead," said Clayton.

"As a doornail," said Pete.

"Hello Allie," I said.

"Here we go," said Clayton.

"Go where?" said Pete

"Back down that road," said Clayton.

"I don't know what you're talking about," I said. I started to make a "shut up" slashing motion across my throat, realized how that would look, then jerked my head for Clayton to come closer.

"Let it go," I said.

"You let it go," Clayton said.

"Let what go?" said Pete.

"The thing with Allie," said Clayton. "Ever since that night he helped her let the air out of Osachoff's tires at your party after high school, he's had a thing."

"There's no thing," I said.

"You let the air out of Osachoff's tires?" said Pete. "I had to drive that jerk home."

Osachoff was a jerk. Allie had come home from university and gone to Pete's party to find her high school boyfriend minus a mullet and plus an earring. Then she saw the new girl from the hair and piercing salon drinking a rye and Gatorade, the boyfriend's favourite drink. Allie didn't need a university education to figure that out.

"My brother the hero," said Clayton, who'd found me holding Allie's hair while she threw up in the ditch. But Clayton hadn't said much that night, not even when Allie cried a little in the seat between us as we drove her home. When we got back to the party, he didn't tell Osachoff about the tire pump in the back of our pickup.

"We only got 15 minutes to figure out who killed Marley," said Clayton. "Don't get distracted."

"I'm not distracted," I said.

"Keep your eye on the prize," said Clayton, pointing two fingers at his eyes and turning around, "Look Allie, we can't leave Marley's murder to those ..."

Allie had stepped over the tarped tree and dropped to her knees beside Marley.

"Don't touch anything!" said Pete.

Allie kept looking, too closely I thought, at the man who'd coached her through firefighter training. They'd spent a lot of time together as Marley showed her advanced fire suppression techniques, safe chainsaw operation, and where to order extra-small fire-proof trousers. When she wrote her final exam, she was the highest-scoring rookie in the history of the department.

"All those times Marley urged me to study," she said.

"Don't look," I said. "Don't remember him like this."

"Everyone loved Marley," said Clayton.

"Not everyone," said Allie.

"Come again?" said Clayton.

"He knew his attacker," said Allie.

"Come again?" said Pete.

"Look at his hands," said Allie. "No scratching or bruising on the knuckles, no defensive wounds, and his glasses are back on his forehead. It was someone he trusted enough to look away from."

"Whoa," said Clayton. "Slow down."

"You wanted to solve it," I said.

"That leaves the obvious question," Allie said.

"Obvious," said Pete.

We were quiet for a while. Then Allie said, "What was he looking at?"

We looked around the firehall. Our road hockey sticks were lined neatly against the wall – except for Clayton's, the murder weapon. Marley's goalie stick leaned against the regulation-sized net, assembled for the street hockey game and, insult over injury, filled with a dozen of the cops' souvenir hockey pucks.

"I've never seen this in the firehall before," said Clayton, standing over the desk where Marley double-checked our bookkeeping. He pointed to the souvenir hockey puck holding open a small leather-bound book with very fine print, some of it highlighted in yellow. A list in Marley's tidy handwriting lay next to it.

"Suppression of riots. Arrest without warrant. False pretenses. Firearms offences," Clayton from the list. "What is this?"

131

"The Criminal Code of Canada," said Allie.

"I knew it," said Clayton. "Marley caught those bastards at something and was studying up on it."

"Marley liked to study," said Pete.

"Yes," said Allie. "He did."

"We got ten minutes to figure out whatever he figured out," said Clayton.

"Ten minutes?" said Allie.

Clayton explained about the float's hitch and Allie said, "Why don't they just unload the snowmobile and ride it here?" Then we heard a four-stroke engine pull up outside and the man I hated threw open the firehall door.

"Chief Osachoff," said Allie.

"Everyone out," said Osachoff. The neckline of his hockey sweater still had the tear I ripped in Game Three of the Township Series. The vee drooped to show a hairy chest and the gold ram's horn necklace Allie gave him the Christmas she deflated his tires. I hate that necklace.

"Kid," called Osachoff. "Get in here."

The Ringer stepped through the door, his face as green as his hockey sweater. One look at Marley and he was on his knees, vomiting next to Allie's tree.

"Get it together, kid," said Osachoff. "We're solving this for Marley."

"We're solving this for Marley," said Pete.

"Chief," said The Ringer, wiping his mouth with the tissue Allie gave him. "I ..."

"Kid, escort these morons from my crime scene," said Osachoff.

"It's your crime scene all right," said Clayton. "There's no way we're leaving Marley alone with the only guy who had a motive to kill him."

"Have you morons lost your minds?" said Osachoff. "What motive?"

"The township vote," said Clayton.

"We're winning the vote," said Osachoff.

"Marley knew his attacker," said Pete.

"Marley knew everyone in town," said Osachoff.

"You had opportunity," said Clayton. "Someone dropped off the hockey pucks."

"You morons have unlimited access to this place," said Osachoff.

"Marley had the Criminal Code," said Clayton.

"He was studying it," said Pete.

"There are only two criminals here," said Osachoff, pointing at me and Clayton. "I know you two vandals let the air out of my tires at that party."

"Prove it," I said.

"You were always jealous of that car," said Osachoff.

"Damn right I was jealous," I said. "If I'd had what you had, I'd have never let it out of my sight."

"Get your own," said Osachoff. "It's called Auto Trader."

"You had no idea how to cherish it," I said.

"I cherished it," said Osachoff. "It was a mint Z-28."

"How do you solve crimes with that pea brain?" I said. "This township ought to be the murder capital of Canada."

I was ready when Osachoff charged at me. I pulled his hockey sweater over his head, repeating my classic move from Game Two. I didn't quite get his arms pinned before he tried a swift shot to my head. I admit he rang my bell pretty good before I got him in a headlock.

"You're under arrest!" Osachoff said through his sweater.

"Stop!" said The Ringer, stepping towards Clayton.

"You're under citizen's arrest," said Clayton and cold-cocked The Ringer.

The Ringer was up fast, trying to put my brother in a headlock but failing because Pete was grabbing his sweater and shouting about citizen's arrest. It was pandemonium; everyone had a piece of everyone. Osachoff and I were in a clinch when we slipped where The Ringer had been sick, stumbled over Allie's Christmas tree, and fell against the switch that opened the bay doors. The doors lifted and we barreled into the parking lot and into the middle of the police pipe and drum band playing Walking In A Winter Wonderland.

Considering they have two strikes against them, being bagpipers and Torontonians, those guys are solid scrappers. Don't let anyone tell you different. They dropped the instruments to stiff-arm their way in and would've made short work of me, my brother and Pete – except that the next float in the parade was Pumper One. Our boys were over the side of the fire truck like they were jumping the boards at the Coliseum. All you could see were fists flying, torn hockey sweaters and kilts that gave a man a lot of room to maneuver. The firefighters were definitely winning. Our Pumper driver delivered a pair of roundhouses to the guy with the fancy baton, while our fire prevention officer clocked the lead bagpiper with his own shoe. I saw Clayton feed two rights to The Ringer, while Pete warned the kilted guy he was pummeling not to trip over a drumstick.

The parade-goers, most of whom had been at the Township Series, were cheering like crazy. We could've gone at it all afternoon. I was barely winded when Allie waded into the middle and emptied a fire extinguisher, coating everyone with foam so you couldn't tell firefighter from cop.

"I hope you're proud of yourselves," she said. "Marley was a good man, a man we grew up with, went to Prince Charles High School with, a man who went out of his way to help people. Now he's dead and you're acting like a bunch of goons."

We stood like melting snowmen, dripping shame and aqueous film-forming foam over the main street.

"Marley would hate it," I said.

"Absolutely hate it," said Pete.

"You're right, Allie," said Osachoff. "We owe Marley more."

"So does his killer," said Allie, looking at The Ringer.

"I'm sorry Chief," The Ringer said, taking out his handcuffs.

"Sorry for what?" said Osachoff.

"I killed Marley," said the Ringer, snapping a handcuff around his own wrist.

"I did not see that coming," said Clayton.

"Me neither," said Pete.

"But you did," I said to Allie.

"I saw some things," she said.

"Like what?" said Osachoff.

"Marley used a highlighter on the Criminal Code, the same way he highlighted the Canadian Firefighters Handbook while tutoring me," she said.

"Marley was helping me study to retake the O.P.P exam," said The Ringer.

"Good for you, kid," said Clayton. "Get away from these bastards."

"But why kill him if he was helping you?" I said.

"Because he was tutoring Marley, too," said Allie, "in goaltending. That's why the pucks were in the net and why he was using Clayton's stick. They met in the firehall so the Chief wouldn't find out."

"You were helping our rivals?" said Osachoff.

"Not really," said The Ringer. "Marley wasn't getting any better. He kept dropping his hands."

"Kept his weight on his heels, too," I said.

"Couldn't track a bounce," said Clayton. "Never turned his head."

"Marley could not keep his eye on the puck," said Pete.

"I swear, I thought he was watching," said The Ringer. "I wound up, took the shot, and just as the puck cracked him in the head I saw he had pushed his glasses up on his forehead."

"You killed him with one shot to the head?" said Osachoff.

"He had no pulse," said The Ringer.

"And you left him lying there?" said Osachoff. "Even these morons tried to resuscitate him."

"I panicked," said The Ringer. "I let you down, Chief. I let the team down. I let Marley down. I'd give anything to take it back." The Ringer started to cry, big sloppy sobs, and a street full of cops and firefighters looked at their feet.

"I thought I'd be happy a cop confessed," said Clayton. "But this sucks."

I disagreed with my brother. I'd only be happy if Osachoff confessed. But I kept quiet as we watched the young man being handcuffed and led to the squad car.

"We did it," Clayton said.

"We did," said Pete.

"Did what?" I said.

"Solved Marley's murder," said Clayton.

"We?" I said.

"Allie's a volunteer firefighter," said Clayton, "so we solved it."

"Allie," said Osachoff. "I owe you an apology."

The big cop took Allie's hands in his, covering her delicate fingers with his paws and rubbing them to warm them up. "You were always so smart," he said. "I couldn't appreciate it when we were kids."

"Uh-oh," said Clayton.

"Now I see things differently," said Osachoff.

"Brother," said Clayton, "just say the word."

"Word," I said.

Clayton jogged over to the snowmobile trailer, Pete right behind. They crouched down beside a tire and started letting air out of it.

"That's police property!" said Osachoff. He cursed and ran, shouting that my brother was under arrest. Toronto bagpipers dropped hot chocolates on the sidewalk and circled Pete and Clayton, and the volunteer firefighters circled them.

I stood on the sidewalk next to Allie.

"Allie," I said.

"Marley told me to study things carefully," Allie said, taking my hand and warming it in hers. "It's the only way to see what's right in front of you."

# Holding Down The Fort

I was a kid again as I stood on the steps of the canteen, inhaling the smells of childhood at the cottage. Noxema and sunscreen on sun-burned skin. French fry grease. Barbecue smoke. The illusion was abetted by the fact that the jetskis were mercifully silent, the only sound a motorboat passing just in front of Poker Island about half a mile from shore.

I was in quest of a chocolate ice cream cone I hoped to enjoy alone as I strolled the beach in a moment of self-indulgent silence. Steve was out on one of his two-hour mountain bike rides and Drew had snuggled up on the couch engrossed in a new comic. If the beach gods were with me, I could nip in to the canteen while none of my relatives were there and avoid another of the long querulous conversations that had been marring our summer vacation.

The beach gods were absent. Aunt Hattie limped in on her cane just as I was paying five bucks for the single scoop cone that had cost my mother a nickel.

"I thought I saw you sneaking in here," she said. "You've got time to come in here and fill your face but you don't have any time to discuss family business."

"I'm sorry, Aunt Hattie," I said. "But – "

"No buts," she said. "It's not good keeping to yourself all the time, waiting for that fancy-pants husband of yours to finish riding that crazy bicycle. Especially now, when we need you. If the Fort is still good enough for you in the summer, then the family's still good enough for you."

"The Fort" is what we call Fort Allen, a fur trading hamlet that bustled in the days when the river was the area's main transportation route. The "hotel" – which serves triple duty by housing the only canteen, tavern and flophouse for 30 miles – is the sole remaining building from the original trading post.

The main industry now is tourism, with summer cottagers paddling their kevlar canoes where the *courier de bois* once glided along the river. A lot of the Fort's summer residents are like me, descended from fur traders who put down roots here. The cottages have been in the family for generations and so we were all caught up, to one degree or another, with Aunt Hattie's new problem.

"Since I'm here, we might as well have a drink," Aunt Hattie said. "Sit down over there."

She gestured with her cane to one of the tables, plywood planks nailed to thick stubs of wood, and ordered a rye and coke from Bob. Silently he brought it to the table, the glass filled to the brim with ice the way she always drank it in August. Aunt Hattie didn't thank Bob when he put it down.

Bob avoided eye contact while he counted out her change. Expecting no tip, he briskly returned to the other side of the canteen's counter. Leaning forward, his burly forearms against the smooth counter top, he watched from a distance as she sipped her drink.

Aunt Hattie nodded towards Bob. "We can't talk about Blind Billy with MacDougalls around," she hissed loudly from the corner of her mouth. "Come over tonight after dinner and we'll figure something out."

"Yes, Aunt Hattie," I said.

The cool evening breeze was coming in from the river when Steve and I paid our command visit to Aunt Hattie's summer home, the pride of Fort Allen's Campbells. Most of the area's cottages were casual clapboard bungalows filled with cast-off furniture. But Aunt Hattie had spent years and every spare penny restoring Grandma Campbell's farmhouse. She had even mounted a wooden plaque on the west wall noting the year she finished the restoration.

Drew hated that place, more museum than cottage. Sand from the beach was strictly forbidden and little boys not much more welcome. Steve and I saw no reason for him to suffer and had sent him off to play with his cousins.

As we walked up Hattie's flagstone steps we could hear music from the hotel next door. That meant Aunt Hattie would not be taking us out to the screened-in porch. Instead, after presenting us with the requisite rye and cokes, she led us into the parlour where a dour Grandma and Grandpa Campbell looked down from their wedding day photograph.

The pine rocker protested as Aunt Hattie lowered herself into it and we took our usual spot on the old love seat reserved for visiting cottagers.

"So," she said. "What are we going to do about Blind Billy?"

It was the question I'd been trying to avoid all the summer and Steve tried to save me from it again.

"Aunt Hattie, what a beautiful little blanket," Steve said slyly. He got up and walked towards the knitted spread that always covered the antique washstand.

He knew the story of the blanket as well as I, but was hoping to distract Aunt Hattie with a recitation of the family history. He knew she always got caught up in the telling, reliving the glorious old feud.

"It looks very old," Steve said, fingering the blanket and wrinkling his nose at the hint of the mothballs which kept it company every winter.

"Old!" Aunt Hattie harrumphed. "That's the crib blanket Grandma Campbell knit for Uncle Harold using those very knitting needles on the cabinet."

Steve picked up the ivory needles that had come all the way from old country with Grandma Campbell's mother. They were a family treasure which I had never been allowed to touch as a child, even though one had long been missing its tip and the pair would never again produce a family heirloom.

"She finished the blanket the very night Blind Billy was murdered," said Aunt Hattie. "She was just laying down those needles when he was brought home."

"Murder?" said Steve, "I thought that was never proven."

"Good Lord, I can't believe she'd tell you the story leaving any doubt as to that," said Aunt Hattie, glaring at me. The Campbells believed there were two sides to the story about Blind Billy, our side and the wrong side.

"Maybe you'd better refresh my memory," Steve said.

Then she motioned with her cane, down the beach and past the government dock where Drew was fishing with his cousins, and began the story I had heard every summer of my life.

"Every time I look down that river I think of that miserable son of a bitch," she said. "There's no doubt Blind Billy was a miserable S.O.B. Many is the time I heard my mother, his own daughter, say that. He was drunk more than he was sober, and he was a mean drunk. That's why they called him Blind Billy, because when he was blind drunk he'd hit anybody in his reach. It didn't matter if it was the sheriff or his wife. That's why nobody believed Dipper MacDougall's story.

143

"It was early in May when Blind Billy and Dipper went off to do some muskrat trapping. This was in '04. It wasn't like the old days when trapping fur was like coining money, but you could still do good from the trap lines if you knew what was what. Blind Billy knew his stuff but he'd lost his boat that spring. He was too drunk to pull it up on shore one night and it washed out in a storm, got smashed to pieces. He'd drunk up all the money from the year before so he couldn't buy a new one, and he didn't have time to build another.

"Dipper didn't know dick-all about trapping 'rats, but he had the best boat in Fort Allen and an eye for the dollar, so they hooked up together. It worked pretty good, until that one day.

"Grandma Campbell started getting worried about dinner time, when they weren't back. Mama was just four years old, but she remembered that Grandma Campbell had dinner ready at six on the dot because Blind Billy always liked to eat at the same time. She started worrying because she knew he'd taken a bottle with him but no more food than an apple and a bit of cheese, and it wasn't like him to miss dinner.

"By ten o'clock it was dark and still no sign of Blind Billy. But there wasn't much she could do about that. She put the kids to bed — all but Harold, because he wasn't born yet — but she stayed up all night by the fire, working on that crib blanket. She was just putting in the last row when she heard the boat pulling up.

"At first Grandma Campbell thought there was no sign of Blind Billy. She could see by the moonlight and he wasn't sitting up in the boat. But he was in there, lying on the bottom of it. He was dead drunk, Dipper claimed. He told Grandma that Blind Billy had got to drinking, saying he'd stay out all night if he felt like it. Then he'd got into one of his rages and started thrashing around until he fell out of the boat. Dipper said he'd hit his head on a rock and knocked himself out and that he, Dipper, had hauled him back into the boat and brought him home.

"They woke mama up when they put him to bed, although they were trying to be quiet. Mama said she heard Dipper say, 'I'll put him down, Edna. If we wake him up he'll beat the bejesus out of both of us.' Then she heard Dipper lift him onto the bed and leave. Grandma was crying a little bit when she crawled in bed with mama.

"The next thing mama knew it was morning and Grandma Campbell was telling her Blind Billy was dead, that he'd never woke up. There was no sign that he'd suffered, just a few drops of dried blood under his ear on the side where his head had been hit.

"Mama said it was at the funeral when her oldest brother Earl found out Dipper was keeping all the trap lines. Blind Billy had borrowed money from him and the traplines were the collateral. That's when people started talking, saying that Dipper had got Blind Billy drunk and hit him on the head. They figured Billy was already dead when Dipper brought him home and that's why he wouldn't let Grandma Campbell get too close."

"Uncle Earl got mad and said Grandma needed money to live on didn't she? He said Dipper was taking food right out of the mouths of her kids. But Dipper said Billy was alive when he left him, that he was a drunk who hit his own head, and that was that.

"Grandma Campbell said she'd get by, that being a widow was bad enough without the whole of Fort Allen talking about her husband's boozing, that she'd rather just get on with it. She never complained, not one word. But the bad blood was there."

She stopped there, but Steve knew the rest of the story. The feud was the life's blood of the families who summered in Fort Allen, even though they had long spent their working lives in the city four hours to the south. It dictated who went to barbecues at whose cottage, whose kids played with whose, who could park their visitors' cars in which driveway. Categorizing families by a dispute that went back four generations was as much a part of our summers as getting one of the Howards from Dog Lake to turn on the water pumps before the Victoria Day weekend.

The feud had been fuelled by the fact that the MacDougalls owned the hotel, bought with money from the trap line. For generations, the Campbells had been forced to buy their ice cream cones and rye and cokes from the progeny of a murdering son of a bitch. But tradition also said that the MacDougalls were tight with a dollar and it seemed part of the natural order that Campbell money ended up in MacDougall hands. The MacDougalls, for their part, insisted that if the Campbells wanted to drink away all their money, it might as well pour into MacDougall pockets.

Now, as we sat in Grandma Campbell's living room with the dull throb of the MacDougall's jukebox in the background, Aunt Hattie repeated her original question.

"What are we going to do about Blind Billy? The Mac-Dougalls want to dig him up you know."

I knew, of course. It was the talk of the summer. The MacDougalls were expanding the hotel and had applied for a permit to build a beer patio where the graveyard stood. It meant digging up the six bodies there, five Mac-Dougalls and Blind Billy.

Billy had been laid there to save Grandma Campbell the price of a cemetery plot and the family had not had the money to move him after the feud broke out. He had lain in the same spot for ninety years and we had come to regard his gravestone as a constant reminder to the Mac-Dougall family of their patriarch's iniquity.

Now the Campbells were gathering forces, determined to save Blind Billy from another indignity at the hands of the MacDougalls. The law said MacDougalls had to foot the cost of moving the body, but it also said the Campbells had some say in where Billy ended up. The Campbells were inclined to leave him where he was if it bothered the MacDougalls.

The feud might have waged on for another four gener-ations, with Drew telling his children to keep away from those thieving MacDougall pups. But I told Aunt Hattie I'd

147

pay for a new stone for Blind Billy in the Highboro cemetery.

The inscription was of her choosing: "The voice of thy
brother's blood crieth unto me from the ground." Every
time a MacDougall was buried in the Highboro cemetery,
the mourners would have to pass by those words. For
their part, the MacDougalls said they had nothing to be
ashamed of but if that's what it took to get Bob his beer
patio permit, so be it.

Since I was footing the bill, Aunt Hattie said I had a duty to stick around till the week after Labour Day when they
were due to dig up Blind Billy. And so my summer
stretched on a bit longer after Steve and Drew had returned to work and school. I had traded my T-shirt and
shorts for a sweater and jeans when the day of the exhu-
mation rolled around.

I heard the backhoe before I saw it scraping away at
the century of dirt that covered Blind Billy. As I headed up
the beach towards the hotel, I could see the shovel as it
thrust out towards the river, then swung back in to scoop
away at the grave. When I got closer I could make out the
individual MacDougalls standing to the left of the graveyard, facing the Campbells gathered on the right. I joined
my cousins in their vigil.

Aunt Hattie stood watch from her screened-in porch,
Harold's crib blanket wrapped around her shoulders
against the chill creeping into the September air. She
stood alone, peering through her binoculars until Billy's

rotting box was unearthed and his remains hermetically sealed for transportation to Morrison's funeral parlour.

Aunt Hattie did not wait to see the fate of the Mac-Dougall boxes. She called her clan to her house and we obediently headed over. Taking off our shoes at the door, we waited in the old kitchen while Hattie poured our rye and cokes. Then we headed into the parlour where Aunt Hattie replaced Harold's blanket in its usual spot.

A while later we heard the MacDougalls move from the gravesite to continue their family celebration in the hotel next door. I pictured them gathered around the cigarette-scarred tables, having a few rounds of draught in honour of Dipper. When Aunt Hattie and I went back out to the kitchen for more drinks, we could hear them baritoning Loch Lomond.

That's when John Morrison, the funeral director, came in. I'd been expecting John, a pleasant man whose family had been burying Campbells and MacDougalls for years. It was tradition around Fort Allen that all bills were handed over in person and no Campbell account with Morrison's had ever been settled by mail.

"Hello John, are you ready for a decent rye?" said Aunt Hattie. She knew he had gone to the hotel first to present the MacDougall bill.

"Don't mind if I do, Hattie," he said.

She prepared him a drink and made some small talk. Then she steamed back out to the parlour with a tray-load of drinks, leaving me to complete the family business.

"Hello missy," John said to me, scraping forward one of the kitchen chairs. "I'm glad I caught you before you went back to the city." After we sat down at the kitchen table he handed me the bill for Blind Billy's monument.

"There's one more thing," John said, after checking to make sure Aunt Hattie was out of earshot. "I know this sounds strange but I thought you'd want to know."

"There wasn't much left of Blind Billy after 90 years, just the bones. That's not unusual, I've seen that before. But when we were putting him in the new box, I heard something clattering around in his skull," Morrison said. "I thought I'd better take a look and I found this."

He handed me a plain white envelope with the words Blind Billy pencilled just above my name. Inside was the one-inch tip of Grandma Campbell's ivory knitting needle.

# *Wrecked*

**Floyd the Buddhist** was holding my ladder when the cop came in about the stolen car. That's Floyd's thing, being in a place at the wrong time.

"Just another day at the auto wrecker," I said as he passed me the hammer. "Smashed front door, stolen car, missing mechanic, and a helpful Buddhist."

"No worries, Rosie," said Floyd. "When we act out of concern for others we create harmony within our hearts."

If Floyd had offered to nail the plywood over the broken glass for me, he might have created more harmony in my heart – but a woman who runs an auto wrecker expects to do her own hammering. Anyway, Floyd isn't that quick and he knows it. "My true path has too many detours," he likes to say.

Floyd was an 18-year-old in a trailer park near Watertown, N.Y., when the U.S. Army sent him to Vietnam. He didn't decide to come to Canada until he was already in Saigon. He didn't find Buddhism until he got here, Kingston, Ontario, less than an hour's drive north from Watertown.

Now he's practically a senior citizen, Floyd is saving up to get back to Vietnam for some serious Buddhism. He makes cash delivering food for the Golden Dong Nai Palace and I let him scrounge his own car parts from the yard. Taillights, bumper, fan belt, whatever he needs.

"My vehicle," Floyd says, "strives for rebirth."

Last week three cartons of mi do bien spilled over his seats after an Austin Mini cut him off and now his differential was shot. But at least he was there, unlike Gary, my mechanic.

I called to Jimmy, the other jackass who actually works for me, and he strolled out of what he calls the parts department, a block concrete room with pine shelves and a door to the scrap yard. "Any sign of Gary?" I said.

"Won't see him before noon," said Jimmy. "He headed for The Taproom last night with that American from the crusher company, what's-his-name?"

"Carl," said Floyd. "From Pennsylvania."

"Carl doesn't look like he's got a lot of miles on him," Jimmy said. "Reminds me of a minister we had when I was a kid. I hope Gary took it easy on him."

"You can stop taking it easy," I said. "Grab that broom."

"If I take your broom," Jimmy said, "what will you ride home on?"

"Start sweeping," I said, "or you'll ride home on a pink slip."

There was glass everywhere, from the door and the coffeepot knocked over during the break-in. The coffeepot pissed me off most because my caffeine-less head was pounding in time with my hammering. I was happy to let up when I saw the young police officer in the doorway.

I was even happier to see it was Tyler, my cousin Betty's oldest, who'd got on the Kingston Police. Tyler's been a cop for almost two years but I still think of him as the smallest nose tackle on the Regiopolis Panthers.

"Hi Rosie," said Tyler. "Need a hand?"

"I'm done, Tyler," I said, coming down the ladder. "How's your mother?"

"Busy in her garden." He helped me down the last step. "You reported a stolen car?"

"Honda Civic 2002," I said, setting the hammer on the counter. "We don't get a lot of Civics, they stay on the road."

"Made by Buddhists," said Floyd. "Enlightened design. Drive one myself."

"Mother of mercy," said Jimmy. I don't pay guys to swear, so Jimmy says that a lot. "You've replaced so many parts you're driving a new vehicle."

"Rebirth," said Floyd.

"Leave the keys in it?" said Tyler, taking out a little notepad.

"You'd have to be Sherlock Holmes to find the guy who drove off in that," said Jimmy. He'd done a little time in Quinte for impaired driving and, while he's been in AA long enough to steer clear of the Taproom and Americans with travel expenses, he doesn't like cops. Not even a cop who liked hot dogs in his Kraft Dinner when he was in Grade Four.

"Someone stole a car we crushed," I said.

"Worth a lot?" asked Tyler.

"Crushed steel is $130 a ton and a car is about a ton and quarter," Jimmy said. "So, not much, on a cop's salary."

"I really called about this," I said. I bent down, opened the safe below the counter, took out the item I'd wrapped in an oily rag, and handed it to Tyler. He unwrapped it, careful of his uniform, although he smudged his sleeve when he saw what it was.

"That's a Russian-made Makarov semi-automatic pistol," said Floyd. "Few moving parts but lots of stopping power."

We stared at Floyd.

"What?" he said. "I was in 'Nam."

"Where'd the gun come from?" said Tyler.

"Russia," said Floyd. "I just said."

"How did it get in your safe?"

"I put it there," I said. "Jimmy found it checking the yard after the break-in." I'd thought of wiping off his prints and saying I found it, but his record was for impaired and I watched enough TV to know about destroying evidence.

"Don't you people watch TV?" said Tyler. "That's destroying evidence."

"Mother of mercy," said Jimmy. "You won't bother with prints for one lousy crushed car."

"How did you notice one car was missing?" said Tyler.

"Because, unlike some people, I'm not an idiot," said Jimmy.

"That's debatable," I said. "But anyone could see. We stack the crushed cars five deep and someone tipped off the top two to get to the Civic. He found the gun there."

"I'll need a look," said Tyler. He took the ammunition clip out of the gun, put both pieces in the rag, put the rag back in the safe and closed the door, double-checking it was shut. I was proud of him. He was very professional.

"I'll come, too," I said. I wasn't sending Jimmy out alone with a cop, not even the Grade Two knock-knock joke champion of St. Paul's School. Of course Floyd wanted to come, but I'd been enlightened enough for one day so I sent him on a coffee run.

"Don't forget the doughnuts," said Jimmy. "Officer Friendly might like sprinkles."

"I recommend a decaf Sumatran blend and apple fritter," Floyd said. "Small pleasures expand our inner life, reducing stress and loneliness."

"No, thanks," said Tyler. "I'm good."

I locked the plywood-covered door behind Floyd as he left. We heard the high-pitched squeal of his differential pulling out as we walked through the parts department and into the yard.

"How are you liking the police?" I asked Tyler, as we headed towards the crusher.

"Good," he said.

"Excellent pension plan," I said. "It's good you got on so young."

Tyler smiled, like all boys smile at the thought of retiring. He said, "Why are all these cars spray-painted with an X?"

"We play a giant game of ticktacktoe," said Jimmy.

"Those are ready to crush," I said. "We mark them with an X after we strip out parts we can sell."

"You don't strip everything?" said Tyler.

"He is a detective," said Jimmy.

"Supply and demand," I said. "If there are 20 Honda Civic differentials on the shelf, we don't need more. We remove the gas tank but everything else gets crushed, steering wheels, seats, whatever. Adds to the tonnage. More weight, more money."

"Money is good," said Tyler.

"You bet," I said. "This is where he found the gun."

We'd reached the crusher, a rectangular, safety-orange box on wheels, as wide and long as a flatbed. It looked a bit like a freight car with the two long sides missing because those walls were down in the crushing position.

"Not what I pictured," said Tyler.

"It's not Barbie's dream car crusher," said Jimmy. He was trying too hard.

"Crushers are built to fit a truck trailer and towed to different yards," I said. "We rent it twice a year."

"Can anyone operate it?" asked Tyler.

"Anyone with a half a brain," said Jimmy. "So not a cop."

"Half a brain is all you need," I said, "because Gary and Jimmy ran it yesterday. The crusher operator didn't get here until almost closing and I lose money every day it doesn't run. Show him, Jimmy."

Jimmy couldn't resist showing off, even to a cop. He made it sound like landing a 747, starting with the safety equipment and going on about the bells and whistles. After he turned on the machine I couldn't hear him over the roar but Tyler kept nodding. That kid was always a good listener and he looked keen as Jimmy raised the walls of the crusher and cut the engine. We looked down into the bed of the crusher.

"Mother of mercy," said Jimmy.

There was my missing mechanic, dead on the floor of the crusher, every bone in his body smashed to bits.

You see some sad things at an auto wrecker. All those car accidents, scarred faces and permanent limps, fathers with brain injuries, paralyzed teenagers. Families driving on bald tires, floor boards showing through when a mother buckles in the baby seat. People working flat out but wrecked by bad luck, or Floyd's karma. It's a sad reality, but it's a regular sad reality.

Gary was a regular guy. Pretty good mechanic, bit lazy on Fridays. Took his holidays during deer season. Liked

Merle Haggard. Bought his wife NASCAR TV trays for their anniversary. And a loaded gun had been found next to the machine that crushed him to death.

"Step back," Tyler said, putting one hand out like a crossing guard, the other reaching for the radio on his shoulder.

That's when Carl stepped out from behind a forklift, pointed a gun at us, and smoothed his tie. He said, "I'd appreciate it if you all put your hands on your heads."

"Carl, stop fooling around," said Jimmy. "We need an ambulance."

"Gosh, sorry, but you don't," said Carl. "Gary's been dead ages." His gun never wavered as he walked towards us and we put our hands up. I was starting to think he wasn't a crusher operator and maybe not even American.

"No problem," said Tyler. "Let's take it easy."

"Super," Carl said. "Rosie, please get the officer's gun and handcuffs."

I tugged at the handcuffs until Carl made a motion for Tyler to help. Tyler carefully unhooked them and handed them to me, then the gun.

Carl took Tyler's gun but left the handcuffs with me. He said, "Snap that bracelet on the officer's wrist. Good. Now, lock the other on Jimmy's wrist."

"Hold up, Jimmy," I said. "You and Tyler should face the same way."

"Never thought I'd see the day," said Jimmy, turning around. "Chained to The Fuzz."

"Now," said Carl. "Where's the gun?'

"You have my gun," said Tyler.

"Don't get smart with me, mister," said Carl.

"No danger of that," said Jimmy.

"What gun?" said Tyler. He sounded puzzled. "I'm here about a stolen car."

Carl mulled that over. He walked to the crusher bed and glanced in, then looked back at Tyler. He said, "I want all the parts from that darn Honda Civic I stole last night."

"All this for a crushed car?" I said. "I'd have given you the damn thing."

"Teeny problemo at the border," said Carl. "If I'd got here before the car was squashed, well, woulda-coulda-shoulda."

"What the hell are you looking for?" asked Jimmy.

"All you need to know," said Carl, "is that I'm still looking. It wasn't in the crushed car and I know Gary didn't have it."

I wondered how he was so certain about Gary and felt my stomach churn.

"What about you, Jimmy? Did you perchance find it?" said Carl.

"Perchance?" said Jimmy.

"When he finds anything, I know," I said. "He comes running in like he's four years old and it's Christmas morning."

"Maybe you both have it," said Carl.

"Would I call the cops?" I said. "And if I did, would they send a kid?"

"She's got a point, sir," said Tyler. "So let's find your part and you can be on your way."

"Sounds fair," said Carl. "But any funny business and I shoot the policeman first."

He tossed Tyler's gun into the crusher bed. I was grateful for the roar when he turned on the machine. I couldn't hear Gary's already broken bones grinding into scrap.

Back in the office, I set my fingers on the keyboard and thought email, instant message, direct message. Carl pulled out the cable and said, "No outside line."

"I'll have to use the backup file," I said, sorry I hadn't sprung for wireless. "It'll take a while."

"Cheap piece of crap," said Jimmy.

As the cheap piece of crap chugged away, giving us a few more seconds, I considered the options. If I said yes we sold a part from the Civic and gave up the buyer's address, Carl would kill us, starting with Tyler. If I said no parts were sold, he'd kill us, starting with Tyler. If I tried to pass off a part from a different Civic, well, it led down the same path. I was about to go to pieces when the squeal of a faulty differential pulled into the front lot.

"Shhh," said Carl, bringing the gun an inch from Tyler's head.

"Is that necessary?" said Jimmy. "The kid's just standing there."

"It's OK," said Tyler.

"Zip it," said Carl, digging the gun, hard, into Tyler's cheek.

A car door opened. Footsteps crunched on gravel to the plywood-covered door. Someone tried the locked doorknob. And tried it again.

"Huh," said Floyd, back from his coffee run.

I closed my eyes and tried to push an image into Floyd's mind, an empty police cruiser in front of a boarded-up business during working hours. Floyd, please, see what's in front of you.

"Huh," Floyd said again. "And so we pause to consider the doors which appear to shut along life's journey."

Then footsteps retreated, a car door opened and closed, and a differential squealed out of the lot. Floyd's karma was working fine.

My karma, however, was a write-off as the computer spat out its answer. No parts removed, stored or sold. I started the old printer.

"Getting the list of stripped parts," I lied, "to check against the sales ledger to see where they went."

Carl looked at me but his gun was pointed at Tyler.

"We keep the ledger in the safe overnight and I didn't get it out today. I was busy. Because of the break in." I couldn't shut up. The printer stopped and I grabbed the paper. "I'll open the safe."

Carl was turning to me when Tyler held out both his arms, taking one of Jimmy's with him. "Put both cuffs on me," he said, as I knelt by the safe. "I'll be your hostage when we go get the part."

"You are my hostage," said Carl, as I thumbed the combination. "Perhaps I wasn't clear." He smashed Tyler in the face with the butt of the gun, once, then twice. Tyler stumbled back, blood pouring from his nose.

The safe clicked open and I looked at my boys. Jimmy was holding Tyler with his free arm, an arm that lifted thousands of parts from hundreds of cars, an arm that had no trouble with the smallest nose tackle on the Regi football team.

"Carl, you better shoot me right now," Jimmy said, "because I'm going to kick your sorry ass from here to Pennsylvania."

I grabbed the rag from the safe and heard pop-pop-pop. Something warm hit the back of my neck. I pulled out the gun, fumbling with the ammunition clip, unable to slide it in.

"Mother of Mercy!"

Carl was against the wall, muddy sludge dripping into his eyes. Tyler had a grip on Carl's gun hand. Jimmy was reaching for the hammer on the counter. They were pulling in opposite directions.

I'd have to bluff with the empty gun. I took a deep breath – and smelled coffee. I realized the muddy sludge was decaf Sumatran blend just as Floyd tore out of the parts department, grabbed my gun, snapped in the ammunition, and turned towards the boys.

"Drop your weapon!" shouted Tyler.

"Like hell!" roared Jimmy, who'd got his hand on the hammer.

"Not you, Jimmy!" I shouted. "Not Floyd either!"

"No worries," said Floyd, grabbing Carl by the tie and shoving the gun under his chin. "I was in 'Nam."

It was late when everyone left, the paramedics, coroner, detectives, reporters, photographers, the people you see on TV who don't look the same in real life. The day went fast, questions, more questions, the phone ringing off the hook. I was too beat to drive when I finally locked the door. Jimmy's wife had collected him so Floyd offered to drive me home before he started his restaurant deliveries.

"I can't wait to get back to Vietnam," said Floyd, opening the passenger door for me. "All this violence clouds my vision of a single human family united by compassion."

Suddenly I felt wobbly, muddled, like I was supposed be somewhere, maybe church or the liquor store. Then I pictured Gary. I threw open the door and heaved until I sat back, wiped my mouth with my sleeve, and realized tomorrow I'd be the one rinsing my own puke out of the gravel. That's when the tears came.

"Good to get that out," Floyd said a little later, cranking down the windows. "Let's get some air in here, deep breathing cleanses the aura."

"That's OK," I said. "I can't even smell the mi do bien."

"You shouldn't," said Floyd. "I put in new seats yesterday."

"New seats?" I said.

"Hope it's OK," Floyd said. "There was an X on the car."

"A Civic?" I said.

Floyd nodded. Then it hit him.

"Let's take Division Street to the police station and see what we're sitting on," I said. "You won't get to your deliveries tonight but it should be the last time I take you out of your way."

"No worries," Floyd said. "The path to enlightenment is filled with diversions, until the diversions become the path itself."

# Cry Havoc

The usual chatter thrummed over the radio as the animal control officer drove a municipal truck up the hill and into the neighbourhood with the barking dog. Someone was taking an early lunch. There was a GPS mapping request for an illegal deck extension on Sparrow-hawk Drive. A Cadillac Denali had been left overnight at the downtown casino and was blocking the employee entrance.

There was a bear sighting in Beacon Hill, too, which didn't surprise Catie Pavlov as she looked out the truck window at the thick plume of grey smoke whirling like a Kansas twister over what the morning briefing described as a six-hectare burn west of town. When she first came to Fort McMurray, Catie was freaked out by the smoke that hung over the city for days at a time, some from wildfires as far away as the Yukon. Now, like everyone else, she was used to it, the acrid scent of burning pine part of the changing seasons in northern Alberta. With smoke driving wildlife from the bush, though, she was expecting a radio call about deer on the only road into town.

Even with the price of oil in the toilet, the big companies were taking hundreds of thousands of barrels a day out of the ground. It wasn't bumper-to-bumper, stop-and-go, like the glory days, but high-speed traffic zipped along all hours of the day and night on the highway from Edmonton, transport trucks of food, supplies, and fuel. Massive tractor trailers hauling two-storey-high machine parts and tires the size of small houses. Add in family-filled minivans heading south to soccer championships, medical appointments, and Costco, and the inevitable collisions meant the road kept its horrible nickname, The Highway of Death. Catie would have preferred bear patrol to deer herding but she still had to pass her firearms certification.

She was getting pretty good at dog catching, especially after practising all weekend in her sister Falen's backyard. Catie was supposed to keep her niece entertained while Falen studied for her yoga instructor certification and she made a game out of looping the lasso end of the stainless steel "catch-em" pole over her niece's stuffed animals. Things got silly when, after a few glasses of Pinot Grigio, she and Falen decided to combine the yoga and the captures.

"Close your eyes and focus your energy flow into your earlobes," Falen said. "Take a long slow breath in. Long slow breath out. Stand up straight. Hold the pole gently, like a baby bird. Feel your earlobe energy transfer to the pole. Now raise your arms and reach out."

Catie was skeptical of Falon's earth mother woo-woo but damn if it hadn't worked. She upped her success rate to 50-50 on the next tries, dropping the cord around the throats of toy animals and gently lifting them into the air at the end of the six foot pole. She was repeating the mantra – earlobes, breathe, stand straight, baby bird, pole energy, reach – when she turned too sharply onto the last street in Abasand Heights and sent the clipboard on the passenger seat sliding towards her. She steadied it with her right hand, glancing down at the photo of the missing man the Royal Canadian Mounted Police had been hunting for days.

Fort McMurray was a young town with an average age of thirty-two, eight years older than Catie. The missing guy was old, fifty-five, with a head of thick grey-brown hair and a beard, last seen wearing a rumpled blue linen shirt with the sleeves rolled up, khaki pants, and off-brand sneakers. He looked like the Bigfoot in a movie she and her Nan watched over and over when she was a kid. He was six-three, had a South African accent, and drove a tiny blue car that he must barely fit into.

Catie had the opposite problem. At five-three and 110 pounds, she looked like the last peanut in the bag on the driver's seat of a full-size V-8 Chevy Tahoe with a moose-catcher grill and full-sized animal cage in the rear. The vehicle felt like a tank, which she appreciated in the winter when the temperature was minus 40 and the roads slippery because it was too cold for road salt to melt ice. The first year she moved to town there were eight inches of snow left on the ground this early in May.

Not today. It wasn't even noon and the temperature was already 30 degrees Celsius and heading towards a record high. She had switched on the truck's air conditioning because she was sweating in the thick pants animal control officers wore for protection from bites and scratches. Some of the parking enforcement boys showed up at the morning briefing in their summer shorts.

Even with the window closed and the air conditioning full blast, Catie didn't need to check the house number. Constant barking had strained the dog's voice box, giving it a high, painful pitch that the smoke was no doubt making worse. It was criminal the way some people treated pets, Catie thought as she turned down the radio and opened the driver's door. The truck cab was two feet from the ground and she pictured herself a superhero plummeting from the sky, landing crouched with one knee to the ground, one arm pulled back to her side, the other fully extended, both fists clenched and punch-ready. She didn't do it. It would look silly without a cape.

"Cry havoc," called a woman from the veranda of the house next door to the barking dog. She wore sensible shoes, faded jeans, a CBC Radio T-shirt, and had not combed her short, spiky hair.

"Excuse me?" said Catie, the heels of her black Doc Martens kicking up dust as she walked over to the neighbour.

"Cry havoc," said the woman. "Let slip the dogs of war."

"Um, hello," said Catie, holding out a business card. The patch on her tan-and-green uniform branded her as municipal bylaw enforcement but her Nan had told her handing over a card looked professional.

"A dogcatcher named Pavlov?" said the woman, smiling. "What an interesting example of nominative determinism. You have no doubt heard a myriad of remarks linking your profession with the famous behavioral scientist."

"I hear a lot of spit jokes," said Catie, who learned the hard way that every university in the country taught a first-year psychology course about the guy who made dogs salivate when a bell rang. "And everyone knows somebody with a job that matches their name."

"I am acquainted with a police officer named Constable," said the woman.

"At least my name's not Crooke," said Catie.

"Or Trollope," said the woman, who seemed to find that funny.

"And your name is?" said Catie.

"Eleanor Wright," said the woman. "Oh, how amusing. I suppose that could be interpreted as indicative of its own peculiar determinism."

"Sure," said Catie. "Do you know the dog's name?"

"In keeping with our theme," said Ms. Wright, "I call him Mr. Barker. I don't know what moniker the poor beast's owner bestowed. I have never heard it uttered."

Ms. Wright was some kind of stunned, as Nan would say, but it was the right kind of stunned. Usually with a barking dog, the neighbours were frothing at the mouth. McMurray was a working town, 12-hour shifts, four-days-on/four-days-off, with a quarter of the town asleep at any time. Catie had heard more than one sleep-deprived worker, red-eyed and bed-haired, threaten to end the barking with their hunting rifle. As far as she knew, no one ever followed through.

"I looked over the fence and could not see a water bowl," said the woman.

"How long has he been out there?" said Catie.

"He was vociferously vocalizing disapproval of his condition when I arrived home this morning on the first flight from Calgary."

Catie pulled out the little black notebook she carried in her cargo pants pocket. Her cell phone had cut out a few times when she was on a call so she kept paper notes now, which her Nan said would never let her down.

"How many people live there?" asked Catie.

"Only the owner is in residence," said Ms. Wright. "There was formerly a girlfriend, her brother, and the brother's companion sharing accommodation. The brother received a redundancy notice and disembarked for other employment, and the sister and the friend decamped with him."

Catie wrote "One resident." Two years before, during the boom, the building inspectors in Catie's unit couldn't keep up with new construction. Now laid-off trades workers were hopping into F-150s they could no longer afford and leaving town, many abandoning pets along the road.

"The owner can be absent for lengthy periods," said Ms. Wright. "He also makes frequent use of his all-terrain vehicle."

Catie wrote down "Away a lot" and "ATV."

"The city placed substantial concrete barriers at the entrance to the trail and posted notices that it was pedestrian only," said Ms. Wright. "Some scofflaws attached tow chains to their large trucks and dragged back the barriers. The subsequent increase in motorized traffic has caused significant damage to the walking paths."

Catie wrote "Look up scofflaw." Even over Mr. Barker's yelps, she could hear ATVs zipping back and forth on the trail ringing the neighborhood, the boreal forest starting 50 yards away, millions of acres stretching north to the Yukon and west to British Columbia, nothing in between but trees, dirt, deer, and bears. The smoke from the fire had not discouraged ATV traffic. In fact, people were driving out for a closer look at the helicopters scooping giant buckets of water from the river to unload on the flames.

The gawkers would fill a hockey sock full of idiots, Nan would say.

"I previously made a report to municipal officials," the woman said apologetically, as if enforcing bylaws was some sort of character flaw. "He left a severed deer head on his driveway for a month before Christmas. The dog barked like the dickens but the sticking point was the children in the house across the lane. They thought it was a reindeer and were inconsolable."

"Classy," said Catie. She wrote down "Gun" and "Hunter." That described three-quarters of the population of McMurray.

"I am the only person on the street without weapons or back-country transportation," Ms. Wright said. "When the zombie apocalypse arrives my survivalist neighbours will no doubt use me as bait."

"No doubt," said Catie. "I could leave a ticket but that won't stop the dog from barking."

"I would be unconscionably irked if something untoward happened to the poor beast in this heat," said Ms. Wright.

Irked was a good word, Catie thought. She wrote it down, then slid the notebook into her pants pocket. "Let's take a look," she said.

Neither Catie nor Ms. Wright were tall enough to see over the six-foot wooden fence. Together they carried a Muskoka chair from the veranda and Catie hopped up on the seat, hoping the head of the union's health and safety committee never found out. As soon as she popped her head over the fence, she caught a whiff of decay, an odour sadly familiar to animal control officers.

"Do you smell that?" She looked down at the woman, who was peering through the fence slats.

"The smoke does seem to be growing more intense," said Ms. Wright.

"Not the smoke," Catie said.

At the sound of Catie's voice, a German Shepherd trotted out from the backyard and down the narrow apron of grass between the house and the fence. It sat in front of Catie and looked up at her with a serious look, reminding her of a framed jigsaw puzzle in Nan's rec room, a dog with a red cross banner wrapped around its chest and standing on a battleground beside a wounded soldier. It was Nan's second favourite artwork, after her puzzle of a donkey wearing a sunbonnet.

"Now, Mr. Barker," Catie said. "What seems to be the problem?"

She expected a barking frenzy but the shepherd sat still.

"He goes still at the slightest attention," said Ms. Wright. "Sometimes I slip dog biscuits through the fence."

"You have a dog?" said Catie.

"No," said Ms. Wright.

"If Mr. Barker stays friendly, and if I can get into the yard without too much ruckus," Catie said, "I could transport him to the shelter and he'd be fed, watered, and checked over."

"There is a gate at the rear laneway," said Ms. Wright. "I assume you have the authority to enter the property?"

"I do," Catie said, stepping down from the chair. "I'll pull the truck around back. Could you wait here in case the owner comes back?"

Catie didn't like anyone watching when she used the catch'em pole. There was no telling how people, even a nicely stunned lady like this, would react when the lasso tightened around the animal's neck. She climbed into the Tahoe, which was already a few degrees hotter. She turned on the air conditioning, even though it was just three houses to the end of the street, and took off her sunglasses because smoke was rolling across the sun like cloud cover.

She was rounding the curve onto the rear laneway dotted with garages when she saw a small blue car parked at the entrance to the forest trail. She pulled in behind, leaving the air conditioning on while she checked the plate, and found a match. She dialled the RCMP duty sergeant on her cell and got a busy signal – not unusual, the duty sergeant took a lot of calls – but the call didn't go to voicemail. She dialled again with the same result, slipped her phone back into her pants pocket, and turned up the radio.

"Is this urgent?" said the dispatcher. "The wind has shifted and we're going crazy with calls about smoke."

"I found that missing car," said Catie. "The blue one from the briefing."

She gave the address, signed off, and rolled the Tahoe forward, tucking it onto the cement in front of Mr. Barker's two-car garage. Leaving the truck windows rolled up against the smoke, she took a dog lead from the back seat, hoping that was all she needed, but grabbed the catch-em pole just in case.

As she walked past Mr. Barker's garage, she peered in a side window to see a typical McMurray "man cave" with a pinball machine and billiard table. A blanket was bunched up on the leather sofa, dirty dishes covered the tikki bar, and the gun safe was open – technically not an infraction because it was empty. It looked like the owner could walk in any moment, take a beer from the full-sized frig, and tune into Bob Izumi's fishing show on the massive television screen.

Catie found the rear gate unlocked, which made her job easier. She could enter a property if an animal was in distress but damaging property to gain access was frowned upon. She pushed the gate open and walked into the yard, careful to shut the latch in case the dog made a break for it.

The backyard was a bylaw enforcement nightmare, with an illegally parked boat trailer, an uncapped downspout, overflowing garbage and recycling containers, three marijuana plants in clay pots, and a dozen other violations. The shepherd stood by the back door of the house, ears forward, legs apart, tail straight, not growling or barking. As Catie took a few steps forward, she saw it was standing guard over two large human feet, one bare, one clad in a forest green suede slipper. The feet were attached to two legs clad in blue plaid flannel pajama pants. The rest was hidden behind a smashed, over-turned teak wood table. The pajama pants and the slipper were splattered with a dark rusty stain.

Her eyes on the dog, Catie stuffed the leash in a pocket, held the pole in her left hand, pulled out her phone with her right and dialled 9-1-1 to get another busy signal. Her hand was shaking so maybe she had misdialled. She hit the emergency call feature. Still busy. Nan was so right about cell phones, unreliable rubbish that let you down when you needed it most. Catie turned to head back to the truck radio when the dog growled at someone standing at the back door just inside the house.

"Please don't shoot the dog," she heard Ms. Wright say loudly through the screen door. "People have grown accustomed to barking but if they hear a gunshot they will become alarmed."

"Then make sure no one is alarmed," said a voice with a South African accent. "Do what I say and there's no need for this gun to go off."

Lord thundering Jesus, thought Catie. If she ran for the gate, the man with a gun would see her. If she froze and he walked out the door, he would see her. There was no way she could get over the fence.

"We will be concealed around the corner of the house," said Ms. Wright a little too loudly while she jiggled the handle of the screen door. "That is how we will remain unseen."

"No shit," said the man.

As Ms. Wright slowly opened the back door, Catie slipped around the corner of the house and ducked out of sight.

"Just stay there quietly," said Ms. Wright. She stepped out the door and Mr. Barker went silent. "That is a good dog. There is no call for shenanigans. This will be over soon."

"It will be over as soon as you find a key in those pyjama pockets," said the man.

"I will endeavour to find it," said Ms. Wright, "and then you can be on your way without fuss."

Catie held her breath and risked a peek from around the corner of the house to see the back of a man wearing a blue linen shirt. His shirtsleeves were rolled up, his arm extended, and a handgun pointed at Ms. Wright, whose face had gone white as she spoke soothing words to the dog and leaned over the body of the dead man.

"I have found something," said Ms. Wright, slowly standing to hold out what looked like a miniature sock monkey with a key ring attached.

"Toss 'em here," said the man. Ms. Wright gently tossed the key ring in the air and Mr. Barker jumped up, caught it in his mouth, raced to the other end of the yard and dropped it in a pot plant.

The man swore. "Enough," he said, swinging the gun towards the dog. "I'm done with this shit."

Catie stepped from behind the house to find time was somehow both speeding up and slowing down. She could hear her breath, in and out, as she stood up straight, holding the pole gently, like a baby bird, transferring energy into it, raising her arms and reaching out. Then the lasso end of the pole was over the man's gun hand and Catie tightened the cord around his wrist, jerking his arm up so that the gun fired in the air three times — BANG, BANG, BANG — as he fell over backwards.

The gun was on the ground and the man made a quick grab for it, Catie pulling in the other direction on the pole. Then he was up, pulling Catie off her feet and whipping her around like a plastic grocery bag blowing in the breeze. She hit the ground hard as Mr. Barker raced forward and grabbed the man's arm between his teeth. The man was screaming and scrabbling for the gun when Ms. Wright hit him on the head, twice, with a broken table leg and knocked him out cold.

Catie got to her feet as Ms. Wright took a dog biscuit out of her pocket and called to Mr. Barker, who gave the man's arm a final chomp before trotting over for the treat. Catie was clicking the dog lead onto his collar when the latch on the back gate lifted, the gate swung open, and a young RCMP constable burst through.

"I'm here to get you out," said the constable.

"You're late," said Catie.

"I haven't even started," said the cop. "Who's that guy on the ground?"

"That's your guy," said Catie.

"My guy?"

"I'm the one who called this in," said Catie. "I found the blue car."

"What blue car?" said the constable. "What the hell is going on?"

"That's what I'd like to know," said Ms. Wright, who had pulled the sock monkey key ring out of the pot plant. "Who is this man? Why did he kill my neighbour? Why is he fixated on this ludicrous keyring?"

"None of that matters," said the constable. "There's no time. We have to go."

"Go?" said Catie.

"The city is being evacuated," said the constable. "Fort McMurray is on fire."

# Kill As You Go

Lally Thibodeaux didn't seem the kind of girl people shot at. Oh, she was different, I'll give you that, but she was a pretty, well-mannered little thing. I took to her the minute she stopped in about renting the old place on the point.

I always thought the point was the nicest spot in the county, maybe the nicest in southeastern Alberta, with the old frame homestead on a rise about thirty feet from the river. Grandpa Allen built it before they dug the well; back then they hauled water up the riverbank. You can see clear down the river from the kitchen window, and there's a fine stand of trees along the banks. There's a nice pasture out back, too, ten acres you could hay as long as you keep an eye out and don't let the tractor wheels get too close to the river bank. It's pretty, gone to tansy and sweet clover. I wouldn't mind looking out at it every morning but the wife says I'm too sentimental. She likes the bungalow we built out near the road after our girls left home. But I liked the idea of renting out the old house. Someone ought to live there, although I wasn't sure Lally knew what she was getting herself into.

She was just a slip of a thing. I could barely see her behind the steering wheel of her big red truck the first time she stopped on our road. She hopped down to ground and pointed her little black remote control, click-click, to lock up her truck tighter than a drum even though the wife and I were the only people for miles.

"We aren't much for locking vehicles here," I said.

"I find you can't be too careful," Lally said. She had a funny drawl, slow and twangy, and looked about the age of our youngest, in her middle twenties. Her sweet face had a tad too much make-up but she wore clean clothes, not like some of those young people with ripped jeans and dirty shoes. She had on a nice blouse and pressed shorts like the women in banks wear and her nails were a rosy pink. I noticed her hands because she was holding the For Rent notice we had put up at Mosier's store in early spring. Since it was into June and she was the first person to ask, we'd likely rent it to her. But for the life of me I couldn't figure out why she'd want to live out there all by herself.

"Are you sure it won't get too lonely for you?" I asked.

"Potable water in-house, clear view for a thousand yards, slight incline to slow progress, and limited access points," she said. "It's perfect."

"Planning a party?" I asked.

"Not if I can help it," she said with a smile. I could tell I tickled her and I like tickling a pretty girl, so I laid the yokel thing on thick.

"We had a family reunion out there on the long week-end last August," I said, hooking my thumbs in my suspenders. "People who were supposed to stay Saturday night were still staggering around on Labor Day. But you can't pick your family, can you?"

"No sir, you can't," she said, not smiling any more, her drawl so strong you could hardly make her out.

"That's quite an accent you got," I said. "Where you from?"

"South," she said.

"A Yankee?" I said.

Lally smiled again. "In New Orleans we'd call you a Yankee for living north of the Mason-Dixon."

"Most people call me a Canuck for living north of everything Yankee," I said. "But you can call me Jim. You sure are a long way from home."

"As far as I can get, Jim."

I fished around but I couldn't get any more out of her. Lally always was tight-lipped. That's another reason I was surprised when those bullets tore the place up. I couldn't believe she'd open her mouth long enough to make anyone want to shoot her, let alone cut loose with a machine gun. We're still picking bullets out of the old kitchen. I found one yesterday in the old radio next to Grandma Allen's pine rocking chair.

You never would have guessed Lally would be mixed up in that kind of a hullabaloo. After she got settled in I dropped by a couple times to make sure she wasn't finding it too lonely and she always kept everything clean as a whistle. Even the wife said so. You could've ate off the floors and Lally gave the old place some touches of her own, although they weren't what I would call girly. First thing she did was put her shotgun on the rack on the kitchen wall. You're supposed to lock away your firepower these days but that rack has been up there since Grandpa Allen shot his first mallard and, anyway, it wasn't like anyone would be around to check.

Lally kept a few more of her treasures on a corner table in the kitchen along with a bunch of wildflowers she picked fresh every day. There was a picture of a small, determined-looking woman squinting into the sun on a cement stoop, gripping a clutch purse in a hand that looked too big for the rest of her. Next to the photo was a black candle in a fancy ivory holder and a crazy statue of a skeleton in a suit. I figured it was left over from a childhood Halloween.

"That must be a photo of your mother," I said one afternoon as I dropped off another of the wife's rhubarb pies. "There's quite the resemblance around the eyes. But she's even tinier than you. Looks like she couldn't hurt a fly."

Lally laughed. "Tell that to the crack dealers who moved next door to her. They never knew what hit them when Mama Marie put the mojo on them."

"Crack dealers, that sounds like a bad neighborhood," I said. "Your mother ought to move."

"She doesn't live there any more," said Lally, her laugh gone. "Mama Marie's passed over."

"You're young to have lost your mother," I said, thinking of our girls.

"I didn't lose her," said Lally, taking a sulphur match and lighting the black candle by the photo. "Someone took her. Shall I cut you a slice of your wife's fine pie?"

And that was all she said. She wasn't one for spilling the beans but otherwise she was a good tenant. She was determined to bring the place up to speed with two hundred amp service and a backup generator to boot. She even put in those big halogen lights to show off the place. Too bad she picked the ones with motion sensors, the racoons tripped them all night. I didn't say anything at the time. I figured when she got done the old place would be better wired than the arena in town and it wouldn't have cost me a cent.

She got in her own electrician and that's when Gord McKillop met her. We thought Gord was a confirmed bachelor. He was a nice-looking lad, tall and strong as an ox, with a good job. One of the Huff girls set her cap at him for a spell but he never took the bait. We thought maybe girls weren't his cup of tea, if you catch my drift. But Gord took one look at Lally and fell like a ton of bricks. He'd find excuses to come by, little things he'd fix for her. Sometimes he'd get a job half-done and realize he needed a doo-dad he had to go all the way to town for, just for an excuse to come back the next day.

It was Gord who found the first voodoo charm. Lally and I were watching him set up an automatic skeet-shooting thing out in the pasture when he found a heart-shaped rock, polished smooth. It looked like the letter "L" had been carved into it.

"Fancy that," I said. "Nature sending you a valentine."

"It's not natural, Jim," said Lally, looking across the field, squinting so her pretty face twisted up. "Supernatural."

"Pardon me?" Gord and I said together. Sometimes we didn't quite follow her accent.

"It's a vengeance mojo," she said. "My mother was a Creole. She practised voodoo."

"We're United Church," I said.

"I'm a Presbyterian," said Gord. "I saw a movie about voodoo. This corpse got up and did the limbo. It was pretty funny."

"Nothing funny about it," Lally said. "Someone put that mojo there."

Gord and I tried to tell her that a person could find all kinds of comical-looking rocks in these fields, dumped off the glaciers a million years ago. But she wouldn't hear any of it.

"Vengeance was Mama Marie's speciality," she said. "People hired her to get back at folks who wronged 'em. She'd hex a husband who laid one beating too many on his wife, or a gang-banger who shot a nine-year-old in a drive-by, or even on the butcher for keeping his thumb on the scale."

"That's one heck of a town you're from," I said. "Don't people there ever call the law?"

"In New Orleans?" Lally laughed but it wasn't the pretty girl laugh Gord and I liked. "The police down there aren't in the justice business, Jim. They're in business for themselves. They don't call it The Big Easy for nothing."

"I saw that movie," Gord said.

Lally sighed and wouldn't say any more. When Gord finished hooking up the skeet thing, she got out her shotgun and went at the targets like nobody's business. She used her little black remote control – it amazes me how you can set almost anything to remote these days – to launch ten targets and she hit every single one. I never saw anything like it.

"Where did you learn to shoot like that?" I said.

"Daddy was a Recon Marine." Click-click. BAM! Another target took to the air and was blown to smithereens. "Every marine a rifleman." Click-click. BAM! "Didn't you pass anything on to your girls, Jim?" Click-click. BAM!

"Are you kidding?," said Gord with a grin. "You should've seen those girls on a tractor. You never saw anybody plough so straight."

"I don't like to brag," I said. "But Laura, our youngest, was Queen of the Furrow at the ploughing match three years running."

"You taught your girls to grow food to make people big and strong," Lally said. "My daddy taught me to kill people with advance reconnaissance and the element of surprise." Click-click. BAM!

I guess I shouldn't have bragged.

Lally shot and shot that day, and all night with the big lights on. You aren't supposed to shoot at night but there's no police to stop you. It takes a big deal to get the Mounties here. In fact, the last time I saw them was when the place on the point got shot-up. They didn't do a hell of a lot then. I suppose we're better off without them. Maybe we are a little bit like New Orleans. Maybe you could call us a little bit easy.

We didn't see much of Lally for a while. She kept herself busy, clearing brush near the house, white-washing the picket fence and honing the points on the stakes so they looked tidy. I thought she went a bit far putting up the electric fence along the riverbank. It didn't do anything for the view. She practiced her shooting, too, until she burned out the target-shooting thing. I watched her kick it one day and haul it into the house. Since I don't duck hunt any more, I got to use the binoculars for something.

I kept an eye on the mailbox, too. She didn't get much mail, just the electric bill and a magazine called Soldier Of Fortune. The wife thought maybe it was about how to win the lottery. When both came in at end of the month, Lally saw the flag up on the box and roared out in her big truck. She hopped out and click-clicked the door shut while I hustled over, and I was just hitching my thumbs into my suspenders when I saw the chicken bones at the foot of the rusty milk can holding up the mailbox.

"Damn cats," I said, reaching down to pick up the bones, which had been picked clean.

"Wait," Lally said, squatting down on her little ankles as easy as you please. She picked up a twig and poked a bone.

"Worried about rabies?" I said. "We don't get much of a scare around here."

"It's a message," Lally said.

"A message I ought to get out the .22 for those cats."

"It's for me," she said. "He's coming."

"Who?"

That's when Gord McKillop rolled up in that disaster area he calls a van, but I didn't figure she was talking about him.

"I'm worried about you spending too much time out here alone," he said to Lally through the van window. "You deserve some fun. Why don't we go in to town for dinner and a movie? There's a pretty good show at the Odeon that would cheer you up."

I liked the way Gord pretended to be doing her a favor, but he should have had the sense to turn the engine off and maybe even get out of the van. No wonder he was still a bachelor.

"I'm not up for town," Lally said.

That's when the wife came out with a plate of her butter rolls and homemade strawberry jam. The mailbox was a regular Grand Central Station that morning.

"Darn cats," the wife said. She handed Lally the plate and squatted to pick up the bones. Lally started forward but the wife said, "Tut, tut." When the wife tut-tuts, you stop in your tracks.

"Lally Thibodeaux, don't you dare say you can't take those rolls," she said, picking up bones and handing them to me. "This isn't the big city, we do things different here. We don't lock our vehicles, we don't put hexes on our neighbors, and if those neighbors give us homemade rolls, we take 'em and like 'em."

"Homemade jam, too," said Gord, eyeing the plate. "You don't see that every day."

"Lally, it wouldn't hurt you to get out a bit more." I put in my two cents. "Excuse me for saying it, but you tend to mope. A pretty girl like you ought to be out having a high old time."

For a minute Lally just stood there looking at us like we had two heads each. "Are you people for real?" she said.

"Beg your pardon?" we said together.

"What's with the baking and the jam and the worrying and the advice? Why do you care?"

"Don't be silly," the wife said. "Why wouldn't we?"

Lally looked at us, at the plate in her hands, then tilted her head for a better look at Gord. "You people slay me," she said. Then she smiled her pretty smile and said, "I guess I could use some civilized company. Dinner tonight. I'll cook."

Bingo! Gord was thinking. Then Lally said, "Jim and Missus Jim, y'all come, too. I'll make you a real Creole dinner."

"Good enough," says I, putting the bones in my pocket. "With four we can get up a game of euchre. We aren't The Big Easy but we know how to have a little fun."

"Euchre," muttered Gord. "Hmmm. Maybe I'll come by early, finish setting up that generator for you, Lal."

"Why not?" she said. "You could look at my skeet machine, too. The launch mechanism is off by ten centimetres."

"I've been thinking about getting a generator," I said. "We lost power for a week in last winter's blizzard."

"I don't know why anyone with a woodstove needs a generator," said the wife, and I knew I wouldn't be getting one any time soon. "We'll see you two tonight."

I hardly recognized Gord when we got to the point that evening. He had on a clean shirt and a tie and his hair was wet. He had an awful big grin, too.

"Got a little dirty working on the skeet launcher," he said. "Lally let me take a shower and change before dinner."

"Nice of her," the wife said.

I noticed the skeet launcher on the floor by Lally's side table. There was a screwdriver still in the barrel, like Gord had left off fixing it in a big hurry. It looked spotless to me, like all of Lally's things, not a speck of dirt or oil.

"I didn't quite get it the way I like it," Gord said, then blushed. "The mechanism, I mean. Might have to come back tomorrow with a little doo-dad to get her up and running proper."

"You don't say," said the wife.

Lally looked extra pretty. Her nails were a bright red and her blonde hair curled within an inch of its life. She was dressed to the nines in a snazzy yellow suit that reminded me of Jackie Kennedy. Gord thought the getup was for him but I got the feeling she just liked to dress up. It was the first time I saw her having fun.

Dinner was different. Spicy like you wouldn't believe. She even put spice in the rice, and a bottle of hot sauce on the table. Lally ate it down like it was ice cream. Gord made a go at it.

"What is this called?" he said, chewing slowly.

"Jambalaya."

"Crawfish pie and a filet gumbo," I sang. "'Cause tonight I'm gonna see my ma cher amio."

Lally smiled again and the wife smiled, too. "You old flirt," she whispered. "Give Gord a fighting chance."

We were a friendly party, four people sitting around the old pine table finishing dessert – the wife's butter tarts, best in the county – and talking about the weather and the garden and the neighbors. We got up a game of

192

cards and I partnered with Lally to make things fair. She caught on fast, I only had to explain the trump card once, but the wife is merciless with a deck of cards and she and Gord took every hand.

"Kill as you go," said the wife, taking the trick with the right bower, about to euchre us for the third time in a row. That was when the power cut out. The only light in the room came from the black candle in the corner. I hadn't even realized it was lit.

"No problem," said Gord, his face spooky in the candle's flicker. "The generator will kick on in about 10 seconds."

Lally jumped up and grabbed her truck keys from the ring on the wall, tossing them on the table where the rest of us sat in the candlelight. I figured she was telling Gord to take a ride for his half-assed wiring, and I guess he did, too.

"Missing that doo-dad," Gord mumbled. "To get the generator going."

"Un-huh," said the wife.

"Hush," Lally hissed. "He's right outside."

That was when the kitchen door flung open and a flashlight cut the darkness, shining into our eyes. I squinted at the silhouette of an army man, with an army hat and army boots and a big army gun.

"Your perimeter fortifications are pathetic," said a voice with an accent like Lally's.

"I let my defences down," said Lally. She stood back straight, hands at her sides, fingers bent.

"You three at the table, let me see your hands," the man said. We laid our cards face up on the table and fanned them out. Hearts were trump and I noticed Gord had the left bower. It's funny what sticks in your mind.

"Not the cards, you idiots." The man swore. "Put your palms on the table."

We put our hands on top of the cards and looked into the flashlight.

"They're civilians," said Lally.

"They're collateral damage," said the man. "I didn't come all this way to neutralize one witness just to leave three more."

"There's no need to neutralize anybody," Lally said. "If I was planning to testify I'd have stayed in New Orleans. There isn't a REMOTE chance you'd get the needle now. Not the REMOTEST."

The wife and I didn't look at Lally's remote lying on the table. We looked at Gord, hoping he wasn't giving anything away. He wasn't. Good old Gord was staring at Lally, his mouth wide open.

"This is your fault, Lally," said the army man. "Why'd you run to the police?" He said po-lice, like in one of Gord's movies.

"She was my mama," Lally said, "and you killed her, daddy."

"Now Lally, you know the way things go." The man's voice was soft, the same voice I used to tell my girls the rabbits chewed up the pumpkin vine and we'd have to buy a jack-o'-lantern from the store. "Your mama had no business putting the voodoo on me. Psychological advantage is the principal weapon in a soldier's arsenal."

"You beat her for twenty-five years," Lally's voice was as bitter as his was soft. "One day you killed her. You lost CONTROL."

That was when I lost control, too. I must have been crazy, carrying on like some hero instead of a retired dairy farmer. But I was mad as spit at this fellow who took other men's wars out on his wife and his little girl, and I heard my voice say. "You ought to be ashamed of yourself, mister."

"Ashamed of myself?" he said. I never heard a man so astonished in my life. "I'm a decorated war veteran. I served my country with distinction."

"Tell it to the Marines," I said.

"Now you are both out of CONTROL!" Lally said. "Now. NOW!"

The army man was turning the gun towards me and that should have been it, but the wife hit the remote control with her little finger. Click-click.

The skeet machine launched out the screwdriver end over end. I expect Lally meant it to be a diversion, but I must live right because the point hit the army man right in the eye. He screamed and the old kitchen lit up like the fourth of July, sparking and popping and smoking, the machine gun bursting with bullets that flashed along the old tin ceiling. Lally kicked over the table, leaving the three of us behind it. I was glad I never bought that dainty, spindly-legged item the wife wanted from the furniture store in

195

town. The thick old pine stopped bullets, or at least slowed them down, although the wife got hit in the leg and was bleeding like crazy. It was her scream that made Gord jump up to go for the gun. He took one in the shoulder and fell back down. He needn't have bothered, because Lally pulled her shotgun off the rack and blasted both barrels smack into the army man's head.

"So much for the element of surprise, daddy," she said.

The man looked dead to me but Lally wasn't taking chances. She kicked away his gun and frisked his body, pulling out handguns and knives and crazy-looking weapons I didn't recognize. Then she used my suspenders to throw a tourniquet around the wife's leg, pressed a tea towel on Gord's shoulder, and called the ambulance.

"She should have told us," I said to the wife as her blood soaked through my fingers. "We could have helped her hide better."

"You old fool," the wife said through gritted teeth. "She wasn't hiding from him. She was waiting for him."

Then I saw how Lally made her stand. She hadn't lit the black candle to keep that bad man away. She wanted to draw him to her. She hadn't made the old place a fortress, it was a giant booby trap. She had taken her old man's lesson about the element of surprise and done him proud.

I still think we could have swept it under the rug, most of it anyway, but Lally wouldn't take the chance. She waited till the paramedics loaded up Gord and the wife, and I drove off with them for the hospital in town. The county has its own ambulance service for heart attacks and farm accidents and allergic reactions to peanuts. But the police have to come all the way from the city and Lally was long gone by the time they arrived.

The wife is enjoying her stay in hospital. No one around here ever got shot before – not on purpose anyway. She's a celebrity, had her picture on the front page of the newspaper, and you wouldn't believe the people stopping by. This afternoon Gord was in, his arm done up in a sling, and he gave me a ride home after visiting hours. On his dashboard he had a heart-shaped rock with an "L" on it. Gord doesn't believe in voodoo charms but I guess he figures what the hell, maybe it will draw her back. Good luck to him, I say. I wish it was that easy.

# Buck's Last Ride

It wasn't the crime of the century. But Buck Pilgrim decided to act like it was.

He was a better actor than Hollywood credited. He was a down-right Barrymore, acting like a big-shot lawman instead of a cowhand playing second banana to a stuck-up horse. But it was Tom Mix, that two-bit, dime-store phony, headlining the Fourth of July at the Schubert brothers' Palace, on the bill with Eddie Cantor, Fanny Brice and the New York Philharmonic.

Buck's latest picture was dying on the edge of the great white north, leaving him to strap on his fanciest six-gun for a cow-town rodeo on the Canadian side of the border.

Here he was, in what they called "downtown" Calgary, harnessing The Wonder Horse to a ridiculous wagon, waiting on a rodeo clown and listening to a kid honk out a tune with a comb and a piece of tissue paper. All so he could give one measly newspaper reporter the guff about how he would catch a bank robber. He was yakking up everything but *Sherriff of the Yukon*, even though the picture was the reason he hit this lonesome trail in the first place. But Buck Pilgrim was no quitter.

"A wanted man looks for a grubstake," he told the reporter, squinting as he tossed the polished leather harness collar over The Wonder Horse's sleek, golden head. Cowboys were supposed to have hawk-eye vision, so Buck's spectacles were tucked in the pocket of his black duster overcoat, a costume department waterproof that had never seen the Chisholm Trail. "This crook won't come by his grubstake honestly," he said. "A man falls back on what he knows."

"You don't say," said the reporter, who had not bothered to wear a tie and who had yet to take a single note. In the old days, before movie cowboys dressed in fancy boots that had never seen cow flop, every front page from Anchorage to Miami would have trumpeted "America's Sherriff Says Bank Robber Will Strike Again!" Now Buck was lucky to make it onto the Ladies page, where he waxed on about how to build a campfire for a romantic picnic.

Buck had expected more scribblers for the publicity stunt that had him starring in a Canadian rodeo cavalcade like the one in Yukon Sheriff, but the gag was panning out about as well as the movie. It was no Tournament of Roses parade that was for sure, no newsmen from the nationals, no American reporters at all. A handful of local scribblers had turned up to the locomotive shed a few blocks from the parade route — a staging area for the few floats they could muster. Gathered outside the shed was a sad collection of Model Ts, marching bands, and a chuckwagon that looked like it was still being used to haul beans, rice and coffee. The Mounties looked passable with their bright red coats and black horses — they knew how to put on a show — but they skedaddled to the other end of town at the report of a foiled bank robbery and a suspect on the lam, and the reporters went with them. Buck was lucky to get this straggler. He was determined this typical gentleman of the press, with dirty rumpled overcoat, thick black shoes, battered fedora and hands in his pockets, would not escape.

"Tom Mix uses secret Apache tricks to track villains," piped up the kid, a seven-year-old charmer with scrubbed freckles and slicked-back blonde hair, stuffing his comb kazoo into the pocket of new dungarees with turned-up cuffs. He was as adorable as Jackie Coogan and wore a little cowboy outfit, a kid-sized felt Stetson dangling on a string down his back, toy six-guns tugging down a too-big gun belt. He was going to ride with Buck and the rodeo clown in a wagon pulled by The Wonder Horse and play a song on his comb kazoo while Buck made a speech and turned over the Calgary Rotary Club donation to Boys

Town. Never work with kids or animals, W.C. Fields had told Buck. But it had come to this.

"Real cowboys don't need Apache signs," Buck said, tipping back his cowboy hat with his forefinger and holding the pose from the last scene in *Cobb's Canyon Caper*. His head was sweating under his snow-white hat with its gilt cord and tassel, his long legs hot in pristine leather chaps that never brushed against a steer's horn. It was hard to walk, too, in his shiny high-top boots with jingling Mexican silver spurs as large around as a teacup. His cowboy heart beat against a soft green silk shirt that would not last two days on a cattle drive to Wichita and no one expected him to wipe sweat from his brow with a red bandana handmade by an Italian seamstress. Buck knew the impressive figure he cut. He had signed enough photographs.

"Phooey," said the kid. "What kinda cowboy can't read signs?"

"Cowboys don't go looking for trouble," said Buck, running the strap through the near-side buckle on the belly band around The Wonder Horse.

"No one wants trouble," said the newsman.

"Tom Mix shoots the bad guy," said the kid, his little fingers spread wide over his toy holster. "Draw, pardner!"

"A cowboy doesn't draw his gun unless he's fixing to use it," said Buck. With a motion as fluid as it had ever been, if not quite as fast, his open hand floated over the pearl-handled butt of the Colt 45 Peacemaker riding high in his silver-studded, two-toned holster, and then the gun was in his hand. It was the choicest gun he had ever owned, perfectly balanced, a gift from Teddy Roosevelt in the early days, and he made a show of twirling it, the seven-inch barrel spinning like a top. Now, without his spectacles, Buck could not hit a stampeding Wonder Horse. He slipped the gun back in his holster as quickly as he had drawn it.

"Just like a real cowboy!" said the boy, letting out an admiring whistle.

"A real cowboy never looks for a fight," said Buck. "He's a hardworking fellow who rides herd twelve hours a day then looks after his rope and his saddle and his horse. He does his job, he won't be put upon and he doesn't care what folks think."

"Sounds like a lot of work," said the newsman.

"It is," said Buck. "Hard, honest work." Buck had headed out to California hoping to make enough for a little spread with a decent back forty. Now he had more dinero than the stock owners who sat on the balconies of Texas hotels counting acres by the thousands and cattle by the tens of thousands. But Buck fretted about what Variety said about his new hat.

"You should shoot the bank robber," said the boy.

"You don't shoot a man who is making tracks," Buck said.

"Speaking of making tracks," the newsman said, "when's the next train?"

"The Twelve O'clock Flyer," said the kid. "We gotta' be done before it pulls in."

That baked Buck's beans. After *Pride Of The Railway*, the biggest rail outfit in America gave him a private sleeper car to tour the country. Now he could not delay a lousy freight by fifteen minutes. Instead he would drive a prancing Wonder Horse and this God-forsaken wagon past the kids and shopkeepers and local paladins crowded on the bleachers on Centre Street which, as far as Buck could tell, was the only street in town with a real name. He would pull up by the grandstand and the regimental band would play. Then Buck would wave his hat, deposit the kid, the clown, and the Rotary Club grubstake in front of the paladins, and The Wonder Horse would bow, all before the next load of grain shipped in.

Buck could not figure out this crazy Canadian 'burg. A real town, like Abilene, ran railway tracks smack down the middle so rich and poor could pick a side and stay there. Calgary was no Abilene, that was for sure. It looked a five-minute drive from one end of town to the other, past churches and drugstores, telegraph poles, and a Hudson's Bay store. But if you found your way across the crazy river that wandered around the town, the road opened out under an ocean of blue sky, reaching out to mountains crouching in the distance. It looked like the set of *The End Of The Line*, the only movie where Buck got shot dead.

"This is some wagon," said the newsman, leaning over to inspect the bright-blue buckboard decked out with a Union Jack and a sign that said Best Wishes From The Cattleman's Association. "How fast can that pony can pull it?"

"Like the wind," said Buck, who had his doubts. The Wonder Horse had never been in harness but the studio public relations guys loved this gag. Buck leaned in close to snap the traces onto the whiffletree while The Wonder Horse stood like a cart horse and let the kid pet its nose. Buck's old horse, Hank, the one he had ridden out to California all those years ago, would have bitten the kid's arm, kicked over the traces and smashed the wagon to hell. Now that was a horse. But Hank was out to pasture and Buck was saddled with a horse that counted to ten and pulled school-girl wagons.

"When does this show get on the road?" said the newsman.

As if in answer to a director's cue, a tiny convertible draped in red, white and blue bunting dashed into the train shed at top speed to brake beside the wagon. The Wonder Horse started forward, about to twist in the traces, and Buck put a hand on its backside and said, "Whoa, there." The Wonder Horse settled down, swished his well-brushed tail and caught Buck a sting across the cheek.

"Howdy, Buck," said the clown, who geared down but left the motor running. Up close Buck could see that, under the crazy decorations, the car was a sleek, two-seater, green as prairie grass, with little wire wheels and a canvas top folded jauntily back in defiance of the chill. Buck had once gone for a cramped spin down Rodeo Drive with Wallace Beery in a car just like it.

"I'm Bobo," said the clown.

Bobo looked like every rodeo clown which was, now Buck thought of it, a lot like Wallace Beery after he left the circus but before he figured out the money was in villains. Wide face, on the jowly side, big red nose, overdone makeup, cheap, baggy clothes, flat black hat with a broad brim.

"Howdy," said Buck, giving his sensitive smile from *Love Song Of Laura's Canyon*. "The last time I saw Rudolph Valentino he was wearing a hat like that."

"No kidding?" said Bobo. "I thought this was a bona fide cowboy hat. That is the last time I take the word of T. Eaton and Co. — say, do I know you, fella?"

"First time in town," said the newsman, eying Bobo's car. "How fast does that little machine go?"

"Fast enough," said Bobo.

"Fast enough for what?"

"For anything," said Bobo.

The man moseyed towards the car with a look of interest, much to Buck's vexation. Was anyone going to remember who was the real story?

KA-POW, KA-POW, KA-POW! The orphan had taken his cap-gun out of his holster and was throwing make-believe lead at Bobo. At the sound of the toy gun the newsman flinched, slipped in a pile of Wonder Horse manure, and fell to the ground.

There goes Page One, Buck thought. All that palaver for nothing. He tossed the reins over the front lip of the wagon and snatched the toy gun from the boy's hand. "I told you, son, a cowboy doesn't draw his gun unless he is fixing to use it and he hopes he never has to use it."

"Phooey," said the kid, scrambling onto the wagon's seat and knocking over a white flour sack painted with black dollar signs like something out of *Blood On The Wells Fargo Wagon.* "Cowboys and clowns. You're all funny hats and no fun. I want to ride shotgun, like on a stagecoach."

"Be careful, son," said Buck, one eye on the newsman who was dabbing angrily at the horse flop on his grimy coat. "There's a thousand dollars in that sack."

"They put real dollars in there?" said the newsman.

"Canadian dollars," said Buck.

"You don't say," said the newsman. He jumped in the wagon, plopped down on the seat beside the orphan and opened the bag. Then he pulled the drawstring tight and hefted the sack. "It's heavier than I thought."

"You ought to try leaping into a running wagon with it," said Buck, although he could not remember the last time he did the stunt that made him famous. They used stock footage now, cutting in his famous leap so that he still hurdled out of Hank's saddle. The Wonder Horse was too valuable to run alongside a wagon, that pretty-boy horse did close-up shots opening doors and kissing pretty girls in sunbonnets.

"You got to feel like part of the horse," said Buck, planting his spurred feet apart. "You start to feel like that Greek guy with the horse that could fly."

"Bellerophon and Pegasus," said Bobo.

207

"When you feel like you can fly, that's when you let go." Buck took a gentle hop toward the wagon but without his specs he misjudged the distance and his too-big spurs tangled him up. Tumbling forward, he planted his face in the red leather seat and felt his gun tumble from his holster. This is going to be one of those sad sack stories newspapers love about forest rangers who get chased up trees by bears or airplane pilots who fly the wrong way, he thought. Buck stood up so quickly the blood rushed to his head and it took him a second or two to realize the newsman was holding the Roosevelt gun.

"Don't be a hero," said the man.

"Is that a joke?" said Buck.

"Stop kidding around," said Bobo.

"This ain't Hollywood," said the newsman, pointing the gun at Buck's chest.

"That's what you think," said Buck. He grabbed the gun barrel with both hands and the man fired three times, point blank, into Buck's chest. BAM! BAM! BAM! Buck had forgotten how loud the gun sounded in a tight space and the noise bounced off the walls of the locomotive shed like one of Harold Lloyd's flash bombs. The Wonder Horse reared up in the harness, tossing Buck backwards as the wagon bolted out of the shed.

"Let's ride," said Buck, careful of his spurs as he jumped over the door of the clown car and into the passenger seat.

"Hold on tight," said Bobo. The clown could drive, that was for sure, and he quickly gained on the wagon swaying its way down the main street as Buck took off his tea-cup spurs and tossed them over his shoulder.

"He's one lousy shot," said Bobo, nodding at the green shirt, ripped and dirt-covered but free of bullet holes and blood.

"It's a Hollywood gun," said Buck. "Fires blanks." He fished out his eyeglasses, looped the wire hooks behind his ears, and saw the kid crying as he gripped the side of the wagon.

"Stay put, kid!" Buck yelled. "I'm coming."

Buck stood up, both hands clutching the windshield, hoping his boots wouldn't slip on the smooth leather seat. He rose to his full height, his long coat flapping behind him like black wings. He knew what it looked like, like a bird of prey taking flight; the director of *The Stage Rider's Dilemma* said it was one of his best poses. He shrugged out of the sleeves and the coat fluttered away to land on the dusty road behind him just as they came abreast of the grandstand bleachers. The crowd leapt to its feet and the regimental band struck up a rousing song, the music in tempo with the galloping horse. The crowd stood and shouted "Buck. Buck! BUCK!"

Bobo edged the car next to the wagon and the villain turned to face them, the reins in his right hand, the pistol in his left, and fired point blank into Buck's face.

"How many times do I have to shoot you?" he shouted, pulling the trigger until the hammer clicked down on empty cylinders. "Just die, will you? Die!"

He tossed the three pounds of hand-cast iron into Buck's face. Buck clung tight to the windshield and ducked his head like the stuntman had shown him in *Fight At The Tumbleweed Saloon*, but the glancing blow smashed one of the lenses in his eyeglasses. The gun fell and landed under the back wheel, sending the car swerving away from the wagon. Buck said a word that he would never say in a movie.

"You all right?" said Bobo.

"Drive," answered Buck.

The villain laid on the whip and The Wonder Horse, which had never felt a harsh hand, leapt forward. Foam dripped from its gasping mouth, its eyes rolling with panic as it charged towards the train tracks.

"Easy, boy. Easy there," Buck called, as Bobo manhandled the car back alongside the speeding wagon. The train whistle sounded, drowning out his words.

Buck took a deep breath, put one boot on the window frame of the passenger door, and leapt out to sweep the villain sideways on the wagon seat. His glasses were knocked from his face but he had done enough fight scenes to know when to expect a fist, especially after Harry Carey sucker-punched him in *The Deputy Steps Out*. He ducked the blow, unbalancing the villain, and that was his cue. Buck gave a mighty two-handed push, the villain managing to grab the money sack as he tumbled backwards out of the wagon. Bobo veered around him but the money sack split when it hit the dirt and dollar bills floated up towards the grandstand like the tickertape parade in *The Sheriff's Return*.

The horse ran on, the reins lost, whipping under the wagon. They were travelling too fast for Buck to toss the kid into the car, the train whistle was louder, the tracks dead ahead. It was the last reel.

"Hold on, son," said Buck.

He had one trick left, the one that got him his first movie job for a dollar a day, the one he had done time and again, but not for real, not in years. He stood up on the wagon seat, his hands in the air, and felt the rhythm of the horse as it bobbed and swayed. Everything began to drop away, the villain, the money, the clown, the car, the crying boy, even the wagon. He closed his eyes and felt the horse's laboured breath, the pounding of the hooves, the sweat that wicked its withers. Buck felt the moment when all four legs left the ground and the horse was in flight. He stepped out into the air and onto the back of The Wonder Horse, wrapping his arms around its neck and starting to whisper. Together they turned, away from the train, away from the crowd, towards the open road that crossed the crazy river and stretched out under an ocean of blue sky and into the mountains.

# Liner Notes

Most of the stories in this collection were written prior to May 3, 2016, which was a watershed day for me. That was the day a wildfire burned to the ground swaths of Fort McMurray, Alberta, and took our home along with it.

Two years later, almost to the day, I wrote these liner notes. It was a warm Sunday afternoon, the sun shining, the window open in my new home office. My neighbours were hosting their first communal barbecue, drinking cherry Cokes and eating "Berta" beef and pickled carrots. Someone picked a mandolin. Little dogs barked at big dogs. Kids played in a garden sprinkler. A mom told her son to hand over his toy pistol. "Just put the gun down, honey," she said. "There's no time to be shooting us. We got to get to the bottle recycling depot before it closes."

I like lines like that. I like writing about small towns, forks in the road, and redemption. (Also, you might have noticed, runaway wagons.) In my stories, people are confronted with the unexpected and rise to the occasion, or not, making split-second decisions with no do-overs.

Setting is destiny for the characters who amble through my stories, whether they are Prohibition bootleggers in a Canadian border town, Catholic nuns on a begging tour in 18th century Ontario, or a B-movie cowboy at the Calgary Stampede. Or even a Fort McMurray bylaw officer with a barking dog complaint on the morning of May 3, 2016.

That idea, of being in the place you are meant to be, went bone deep on Wolfe Island, Ontario, where I grew up. I find it easy to set a story there — although, it must be said, in reality, the place has never seen a murder. The last crime I recall reported to the police was the theft of a decorative windmill from a front lawn. (I know whodunnit. But forget it, coppers. I'm no rat.)

I called this anthology Kill As You Go, a phrase from the card game euchre, which was played as a blood sport on the Island. There were no stakes except bragging rights, families played together, and our elders were particularly ruthless. "Kill as you go," someone would say as they took all the tricks and euchred their favourite grandchild. It means never let an opportunity go to waste, come out strong, and take your knocks when the deal doesn't go your way.

Kill as you go.

Therese Greenwood
May 2018

# About the Author

Therese Greenwood's short fiction has appeared across Canada and in the U.S. in such publications as the Crime Writers of Canada's *Over The Edge* anthology and *Ellery Queen Mystery Magazine*. She has twice been short-listed for the Arthur Ellis Award, Canada's top mystery writing prize, and has co-edited two short crime fiction anthologies. She grew up on Wolfe Island, Ontario, the largest of the Thousand Islands, and the region forms the backdrop for much of her fiction. She also writes about Fort McMurray, Alberta, where she now lives with her husband. Visit her online at **www.therese.ca** and **@WolfeIslander** on Facebook and Twitter.

**COFFIN HOP PRESS**
New Crime. New Weird. New Pulp.

Visit us online at
www.coffinhop.com